PRAISE FOR PREVIOUS NOVELS IN THIS SERIES

SEIZURE

From the beginning of *Seizure*... the reader is captivated by its skillfully sewn plot.

Amazon review

A wonderful thriller

I really enjoyed this page-turner, which takes the reader across the globe with detailed descriptions of different places and cultures. The nuanced mix of medicine, human nature, international intrigue, and family is well done, and it would also make a great movie, too.

Amazon review

Edge of your seat medical thriller

This is a wonderful read, one of those can't put it down books. I'll admit I'm a sucker for high tech medical thrillers, and this was cutting edge. Once the ball starts rolling in this story, it's non-stop tension until the end.

Amazon review

A terrific read! I couldn't put it down. It's well-paced, with just the right amount of twists and turns to keep the reader on her toes and turning those pages.

Writer's Digest

This book is exemplary in its structure, organization, and pacing...unique but still has strong appeal for most readers in its intended genre. All main characters (including antagonists) are ... fully fleshed out with compelling, layered motivations and traits. Secondary characters are unique and have meaningful purpose.

Writer's Digest

DEATH BY DENIAL

A must read

Awesome book and great read

Amazon review

Medical thriller executed with deft skill and precision Peter Black, an accomplished physician, calls upon these skills as his hero Dr. Duncan "Mac" MacGregor finds his first-hand knowledge of COVID needs to be heard. Instead, he finds himself on another adventure-filled journey with plot twists and obstacles until the book's conclusion.

Amazon review

BERSERKER

Great action in a hot political topic

This book presents a hard-driving account of the dangers of domestic terrorism in the Unites States. Using a Viking drug, insurrectionists plan to destabilize the country. Dr. Mac MacGregor and his team must anticipate and block their disastrous plan. The book kept me up most of the night. Wonderful read.

Amazon review

不怕
NOFEAR

Fiction by Peter Black

Seizure

Death By Denial

Berserker

NoFear

Non-Fiction by Peter Black

Living with Brain Tumors (with Sharon Hogan)

An Introduction to Neurosurgery (with Eugene Rossitch, MD)

Astrocytomas: Diagnosis, Management, and Biology (with William Schoene, MD and Lois Lampson, PhD)

Secretory Tumors of the Pituitary Gland (with Nicholas T. Zervas, MD, E. Chester Ridgway, MD, and Joseph B. Martin, MD)

Angiogenesis in Brain Tumors (with Matthias Kirsch, MD)

The Surgical Art of Harvey Cushing

Harvey Cushing at the Brigham (with Matthew Moore, MD, and Eugene Rossitch, MD)

Operative Neurosurgery (with Andrew Kaye, MD)

Cancer of the Nervous System (with Jay Loeffler, MD)

Minimally Invasive Neurosurgery (with Mark Proctor, MD)

Meningiomas (with Necmettin Pamir, MD, and Rudolf Fahlbusch, MD)

Core Techniques in Operative Neurosurgery (With Rahul Jandial, MD, and Paul C. McCormick, MD)

Functional Imaging: An Issue of Neurosurgical Clinics (With Alexandra Golby, MD)

Website: peterblackbooks.com

不怕

NOFEAR

DR. DUNCAN MACGREGOR THRILLER
NUMBER FOUR

PETER BLACK

Skean Dhu Press
Cambridge, Massachusetts

SKEAN DHU

Skean Dhu Press
Cambridge, MA
Skeandhupress.com

Cover and text design by Mayapriya Long, Bookwrights

ISBN: 978-1-952683-14-5, paperback
ISBN: 978-1-952683-15-2, hardbound
ISBN: 978-1-952683-16-9, ebook
ISBN: 978-1-952683-17-6, audio book

不怕

PART ONE

THE ORIGINS OF NOFEAR

不怕

CHAPTER ONE

THE INCIDENT AT THREE GORGES DAM

THREE GORGES, CHINA

Wearing the coveralls and hard hat of a utility worker, Sophie Grainger stepped from the van onto the road that formed the top of Three Gorges Dam. She tried to ignore the oppressive heat of the summer day and the deafening roar rising from the harnessed Yangtze River.

The van driver held up two fingers. Two minutes. No longer. She had used all her cash to bribe him, pretending she was an enthusiastic American who ached to see the world's most powerful hydroelectric facility up close.

She nodded and moved to the edge of the roadway. The open sluiceways below created water jets fifty meters long as they decompressed the summer surge of China's largest river. Despite the time pressure, her thoughts turned to the fear and sadness that led her here. Her heart pounded in her ears, and she wondered if she had in fact chosen the right solution to her crippling anxiety.

The filthy spray slapped her back to attention. A car pulled behind her van. She had to move fast.

Holding onto the guard rail at the edge of the roadway, Sophie leaned forward to jump to her death.

A powerful hand clamped her wrist from behind.

Shocked, Sophie wheeled around to see who had dared touch her.

A tall Asian stranger towered above her, staring down at her with hard unblinking eyes.

She pushed off from the edge of the dam despite him.

Her five-foot-three frame dangled like a rag doll over the abyss while the man kept her suspended, bracing himself against the railing.

"Let me go," Sophie shouted. Her right shoulder screamed with pain as the arm took all her weight and seemed about to dislocate from its socket. As she writhed and twisted, she saw dam workers stare, mobilize their smart phones, take videos, or call for help. The van she had taken to get here disappeared into the distance.

Holding her wrist with both his hands now, the stranger pulled her back through the rails and dragged her along the edge of the roadway. "What's going on? Release me. I'm an American," she shouted, trying to gain her footing.

The stranger said nothing.

She scrabbled to her feet but still could not stop his relentless forward momentum. "Who are you?" Sophie shouted. "Where are you taking me?"

Again, no response. In desperation, she shouted "Help! This man is kidnaping me!"

The man flashed an ID badge at the cluster of workers gathering around them. They all melted back and watched in silence. No one moved to assist her.

Pulling herself forward, she grabbed her assailant's arm and tried to bite his wrist, tasting only the cloth of his suit and shirt sleeve.

He stopped, turned, and slapped her face with the back

of his free hand. Her head snapped back, and her hard hat flew off. Dots of light filled her vision. She tasted blood.

Yanking her arms behind her, he fastened handcuffs to both her wrists, ignoring her screams of pain as her sore shoulder stretched.

Now he pushed her ahead of him instead of pulling her, prodding her toward a black vehicle parked at the side of the road.

"What are you trying to do? I'll report you to the police," Sophie sobbed.

"Do not waste your time," he suddenly said in good English. "The police report to me."

She turned, stopped, and stared at his unexpected speech. Chinese male, forty, clean-shaven, well-fitting suit, white shirt and tie. Looked more like an official than an abductor. But why would he prevent her suicide and then kidnap her? And where did he come from?

He pushed her toward the limousine, with a driver now standing beside it.

Sophie recognized the car as a Hongqi HQ9, used primarily by Communist Party leaders. She pulled away and tried to run. Wrists still handcuffed behind her, she lost her balance and fell onto the road, twisting her body just in time to avoid falling on her face.

She struggled to get up again but could not even pull herself to her knees with her arms fastened behind her. Sweat dripped into her eyes. She felt as if she would explode with anxiety.

The man watched her flail for a few minutes, then pulled her to her feet and pushed her toward the car. The driver opened the back door, revealing a net where the seat belt should be. The stranger removed Sophie's handcuffs, refastened them with her arms in front of her, pushed her onto the rear passenger seat, strapped the webbing across her chest, and climbed into the back seat beside her.

Sophie sat with tears rolling down her face as the driver maneuvered the car off the dam and onto the highway. Were they returning to Yichang? Was she going to be brutalized? Was this the terrible end of her miserable experience in China?

"Please tell me what you're going to do," Sophie sobbed. "You have no idea what I've been through. Who are you?"

"My name is Jin," the man said without raising his voice, looking straight ahead. "I work for the Party. You are Sophie Grainger, Ph.D., thirty-five years old, an American chemist who entered China on a government grant to study traditional medicine. No living parents, no children, no husband after a painful divorce. Grant and visa terminated early by the Chinese government three weeks ago. No funds to get back to the States and nowhere to go even if you had money. No way to stay in China. No job, no future. Suffering from acute anxiety and depression. This morning, bribed a utility worker and travelled with him in his van from Yichang to kill yourself in the sluiceways of Three Gorges Dam."

"How do you know all this?" Sophie asked, staring at Jin, her eyes now dry but a new kind of terror rising within her. She noticed that the traffic along the road pulled over as their vehicle overtook them. Whatever or whoever Jin was, he had serious privilege.

"We have watched you for some time."

"*We?* Who are we?"

"My people. I was the one who followed you here, but we have been tracking you for weeks."

Sophie considered the implications of that statement. Was

Jin somehow involved in the government withdrawal of her grant funding? Was he the reason she had been running on a level of anxiety and depression she could barely tolerate?

She might die right in front of him from a heart now racing out of control. For weeks, she had been watched and followed.

"You have just trespassed in a forbidden zone," Jin said. "That is punishable by jail."

He waited while terror built within her. Imprisoned in a remote region of Western China. No American consulate to help her, no rights. Probably no limit to the term of her incarceration. She had heard stories of expatriates held for years in jail without any chance of reprieve.

Sweat dripped into her eyes despite the air conditioning in the car.

"I am authorized to make you an offer," Jin said. "If you refuse it, you will go directly to prison."

"What is it?" she asked, resistance gone.

"For one week, you must drink an infusion made from these." He laid a packet of long brown dried leaves in her lap. "Grind a new leaf and let it steep in boiling water for five minutes twice a day. One week from today, you must meet me in the tea house at Yichang's Great Hall of the People at ten a.m."

"That's all?" Sophie asked, staring at the packet. "What's in the leaves? Do they have some kind of poison in them?"

"No poison. They come from *Bupa* plants, which grow wild in Hubei province and were once used in traditional Chinese medicine."

"What does *Bupa* mean?"

"*No Fear.* The leaves of this plant take away anxiety. We want to know whether it works for you."

He looked up at the buildings of Yichang now surrounding them. "But we have reached the end of our time. Remember, ten a.m. one week from now at the tea house. In the meantime, you will be under constant surveillance. We will know every move you make. Don't be foolish and try to escape."

Sophie glanced at her watch. The ride from Three Gorges took twenty minutes with this official limousine. The trip in the van had taken an hour and a half, slowed by traffic and other impediments. That more than anything convinced her that Jin was who he said he was and could do exactly what he promised to do.

The car pulled up in front of her tenement, a dilapidated structure in a side street of Yichang.

Jin released Sophie's netting and handcuffs. She stumbled onto the sidewalk and watched the vehicle disappear into the distance. Relieved to be free, but terrified about what might come next, she felt her anxiety rise to an unsustainable level.

不怕

CHAPTER TWO

THE PLAN

TIANANMEN SQUARE, CHINA

Jin reported to his Communist Party boss Han Li three days later, on October 1, China's National Day. They met in the observation room of the Great Hall of the People beside Beijing's Tiananmen Square. Chinese President Zhang stood meters away, surrounded by members of the Politburo Standing Committee of the Chinese Communist Party.

Thousands of soldiers, missiles, and tanks paraded before them to celebrate the day Mao Zedong declared the creation of the People's Republic of China in 1949. The rumble of tank treads, cadence of marching feet, and shouting of the crowds filled Jin with pride.

Han beckoned Jin to follow him to a quieter room, where he spoke only loudly enough to be heard above the marching and shouting below.

"All this military show is useless," Han said with a disgusted tone. "To cripple the United States, we don't need an army. We just need social chaos. If we can engineer that, the country will destroy itself from within. The *Bupa* plant will be our army, and you will be the commander-in-chief."

Jin was taken aback. He had thought the *Bupa* plant he had given to Sophie Grainger would be an accessory in the effort to disrupt America. Now it appeared to be the major weapon.

Han wielded immense power as a member of the Politburo Standing Committee and had the ear of President Zhang. His orders had to be followed.

"You have done well to recruit Sophie Grainger," Han said. "She must start on the extraction and manufacturing process at once. I cannot trust this to an internal Chinese group for reasons I'm sure you understand. No one in China can be trusted. Grainger has the expertise, and the manufacturing facility is ready. We must rely on you to be sure she is motivated."

"Sophie Grainger has no family and no work. She is desperate," Jin said. "I guarantee that she will be ready to begin next week."

不怕

CHAPTER THREE

SOPHIE DRINKS THE TEA

YICHANG, CHINA

Back in her studio apartment after Jin left, Sophie felt her heart continue to race. *What was in the Bupa plant? Why had she never heard of it?*

Anxiety, an old enemy, began to overwhelm her.

She decided to consult a traditional healer she had worked with for months, a woman revered for her knowledge of traditional Chinese herbal remedies. Grabbing Jin's bag of leaves, she rushed to the small storefront. The herbalist, a grey-haired woman bent with age, seemed happy to see her until she spilled the leaves on the desk.

The woman pulled back and looked at Sophie with wide eyes. "Where did you get these?" she asked in Mandarin. "They are from *Bupa*, a forbidden plant."

"Why forbidden?" Sophie asked, working hard at her own Mandarin skills.

"Makes people do dangerous things. Government prohibits using it. It is cursed."

"Would anyone else know more about its effects?"

"No. And do not ask me any more questions. Take those leaves away now!"

Sophie returned to her room, more concerned than ever.

A plant previously prohibited by the government forced on her by a government official? *Was this some kind of slow extermination to get rid of her? What could this mean?*

She realized the answer didn't matter. Jin's options left her with a simple choice—go to jail or drink a tea leaf infusion for a week. If she died because of the leaves' toxicity, that would just finish what she had tried to do by jumping into the Three Gorges sluiceway.

But could she escape into the Hubei countryside and disappear?

Of course not. Jin could trace a single Caucasian woman in this remote part of the country without any difficulty.

And what's the harm in trying a traditional Chinese medication for a week? She had already experimented with dozens of herbal remedies in her research. None of them had any real effect on anything.

She trembled as she boiled water, staring at the bag. Dumping five leaves into the steaming teapot, she waited for three minutes, paralyzed again by her inchoate anxiety. Her heart bounced in her chest as she considered the circuitous route that brought her here. Uncompromising parents who scarred her with a feeling she was never good enough, a post-doc in Dr. Grace Wu's lab in Boston that taught her how to extract active molecules from Chinese herbal remedies, a Chinese government grant that seemed tailor-made for her to study the biochemistry of traditional Chinese medicine...

She had arrived in Yichang eager to go ahead. Only six months later, a few weeks ago, the government cancelled her grant, leaving her without work including salary in a remote city of Western China. Now she appeared to be at the mercy of some Chinese official.

She could barely get the first sip of *Bupa* tea down. It

tasted terrible, but no worse than some of the herbal preparations she had already tried. She found no change in her anxiety, which was now heightened by a fear of imprisonment and the realization that she was being watched.

She tossed and turned all night, felt her heart race without any provocation, broke into a sweat without warning. The next morning, she sat in her one-room flat, afraid to leave, staring at her bed and refrigerator.

She noted no palpitations or shortness of breath as she drank the second day's potion. Perhaps her anxiety seemed less. At least she swallowed the tea without gagging.

When she awoke on the third day, she felt that something had changed. She felt more confident, less afraid. She chided herself for having been so cowardly in the last weeks and spent the day wandering the streets of Yichang. Each passerby, each blade of grass in the park, each car parked by the road, seemed to have special significance. A feeling she had never experienced with alcohol or prescription medicine empowered her and lessened her anxiety. Optimism began to replace pessimism, hope displaced despair, some faint light sent feeble rays into the dark regions of her soul.

The fourth day was even better. She graded her anxiety as a five out of ten, down from her usual nine.

By the day Jin had ordered her to meet with him, she felt energized and eager to face whatever challenges faced her. She felt confident, alive, fearless.

They met in the Great Hall in Yichang as planned. Jin stared at her when she joined him at the table. "You seem to radiate energy. It's obvious you've taken the supplement."

"*Bupa* might be the best thing that ever happened to me," Sophie said. "It's made my chronic anxiety disappear, even though I'm also very nauseous. Why is this plant not available to more people?"

"In its natural form it has unpredictable qualities," Jin said. "It is unreliable. The active ingredient has not been purified, and many people have bad side effects."

He beckoned for her to sit across from him "We want you to create a manufacturing protocol that allows mass production of a compound without side effects. You know the benefits of *Bupa* first-hand, and you know the science. My superiors and I want to offer you a once-in-a-lifetime opportunity."

Creating reproducible compounds from traditional herbs was a skill she had perfected in Wu's lab. She knew well the chromatographic, mass spectrometric, and other techniques needed.

And Jin seemed to have changed from a persecutor to a business associate eager to proceed with the project. He seemed to be offering her a new chance in life.

The only problem for her was staying in China. She had been dumped by the government once. If it happened again, she wanted to be in a country that would allow her to get another job easily. Her Mandarin was passable but not good enough, and she had the feeling that Westerners were going to be increasingly unwelcome in the People's Republic over the next decade. She wanted to have the protection of Western rules if the job didn't pan out, never wanted to be out of funds again.

"Does the manufacturing facility have to be in China?" she asked.

"No. We have already chosen Istanbul, gateway between Asia and Europe. Our facility will be on the European side."

"Where exactly?" The idea of living in what she had heard to be a spectacular city seemed alluring.

"We took over a pharmacology manufacturing plant near the old seaport in Kadikoy. You can live near there and spend all the time you want looking at the Bosporus."

Jin now appeared to be a business recruiter. Sophie decided to continue as if this were a job interview. "What do I get paid? What is my operating budget?" she asked.

"You will have a good salary and a budget to get what you need."

"And my mission?"

"To make a synthetic form of *Bupa* that can be manufactured, stored, and delivered around the world. It should be in the form of a pill. After you have developed the process, we will continue your salary to guarantee the compound is produced according to your standards. We want to be sure we are selling active product."

A good salary, challenging work, new life in one of the most interesting cities in the world. Sophie realized perhaps it was the *Bupa* circulating in her body that made her so confident, but she accepted on the spot.

不怕

CHAPTER FOUR

NOFEAR PRODUCTION BEGINS

ISTANBUL, TÜRKIYE

In two days, Sophie packed up her small Yichang apartment and moved to Istanbul. She found a fourth-floor flat among the jumbled hillside tenements behind Taksim square. Her back window overlooked the Bosporus, and she at once felt part of a vibrant Turkish community, buying pastries and other food as necessary in the shops around the apartment.

She could walk to the laboratory, admiring the brightly painted wooden boxes which lined the cobbled pathways and served as homes for local cats, revered and protected by the Turkish community. She spent evenings on her tiny patio overlooking the Asian coast, watching the constant Bosporus traffic of ferries and container ships. She ate Turkish *mezze*, drank Turkish wine and Raki, and focused on her major goal—to create a marketable version of what she now called NoFear.

Setting up the manufacturing process was not as hard as she thought. The factory Jin and his associates had bought was well supplied. With a small modification she was able to reconfigure the equipment to NoFear extraction and purification.

At the end of eight months, she congratulated herself on creating just what she'd aimed for—a sophisticated synthetic sequence that reduced the *Bupa* plant to an odorless, tasteless, pill.

During that period, she became a dedicated advocate for the compound, taking a pill morning, noon, and night. She found that she had little time for food, even the delicious doner kebab served in Taksim Square. She simply wasn't hungry.

From time to time, she wondered whether she was becoming an addict to this remarkable pill.

She had seen colleagues succumb to the attraction of cocaine, alcohol, even heroin in the past.

But this pill was different. It did not produce a high. It simply filled her with confidence and joy. She viewed it as an aid to focused productivity, not a recreational drug.

Everything changed one morning. Deciding to buy a new dress, she looked at herself in the store's full-length mirror, a luxury she did not have in her flat. She saw a pathologically thin woman with cheekbones like jagged ship prows in a scrawny face. Her hair was stringy and unruly. Her dress hung off her frame like a sack.

"This is not good," she said out loud as she stared at her image. "I need to eat, to slow down."

She decided to stop NoFear.

By the second day without her pills, headaches, nausea, and a feeling of doom overtook her and kept her from any productive work. By evening she could not stand the body aches, nausea, and anxiety that overtook her. She trembled so much she could not write, found sweat dripping into her eyes, felt her heart racing.

She tried to go to sleep and dozed off fitfully but woke

with stiff legs and an aching back. With a start, she realized she had been incontinent of urine, wetting her mattress.

She knew what this was, had heard stories from her graduate school colleagues about this scenario.

She had experienced a nocturnal seizure.

Terrified now, she took three pills at once and stayed up watching the Bosporus lights on her patio, wrapped in a blanket and shivering.

By the morning, she felt well enough to shower and noted that her hands did not shake any more. By the end of the afternoon, she was ready to work.

She remembered some experiments described in her Intro to Psychology course many years ago. Rats had electrodes implanted in their *locus coeruleus*, a part of the brain stem which regulates the feeling of pleasure. When the rats pressed a lever, they got a mild jolt which seemed enjoyable. In fact, the jolt appeared so enjoyable that the rats would keep pressing the lever instead of eating or drinking. After a few weeks they died from malnutrition, still pressing the lever up to the moment of death.

Was she becoming a pleasure-seeking rat?

The idea became an obsession. She dreamed of rodents with her own face pressing the lever until they keeled over dead. During the day, she cursed herself every time she reached for NoFear, but could not stop taking it at least three times a day. She did force herself to eat, filling out her body contour so she looked less wasted.

She began to think about the implications of the compound she had created. It eliminated anxiety, but in the process stoked a dependency that was as bad as any heroin addiction she had seen. *Was she a modern-day Dr. Frankenstein who had created a pharmacological monster?*

不怕

CHAPTER FIVE

SOPHIE MEETS MAC

ISTANBUL, TÜRKIYE

Sophie Grainger had been proud the day she completed the synthetic sequence for the NoFear pill, allowing production to be ramped up for the American market.

Now she was guilt-ridden when she realized what she had done. She realized a decision about what to do in this situation required advice from someone she trusted. From Istanbul, she could easily reach out to former colleagues to solve her dilemma about a powerful drug with addictive properties.

She connected first with Dr. Grace Wu, her former mentor and now a faculty member in neuroscience and neuropathology at Harbor Hospital in Boston. Sophie had done a postdoc in Wu's laboratory, learning the analytic and synthetic techniques needed to create a psychoactive compound from a plant product. It was Wu who had encouraged her to study traditional Chinese medicine as the next step, and that led to the grant that had taken Sophie to China.

"I'm sorry your Yichang project got cancelled," Wu said when Sophie called her, "but I'm delighted you moved to Istanbul. You're more a part of the scientific community there."

"Can I ask you something?" Sophie asked. "I'm involved in the manufacture of a new drug that removes anxiety. One of the early test subjects tried to stop taking it suddenly and had a seizure. I'm convinced the compound is addictive. What should I do?"

"In the States," Grace said, "you'd have to report your concerns to the Food and Drug Administration. I don't know whether a similar regulatory agency exists in Turkey and if so, what the procedure would be."

"But leaving the government aside, what's the right thing to do?" Sophie pressed her.

"You should at least do further testing before it goes on the market. But I have a suggestion," Grace said. "One of my best friends will be at the Hilton Istanbul Bosphorus next week to attend a World Congress of Neurosurgery. He has a background in both neuroscience and medical ethics. You should talk to him while he's there. Maybe he can help."

"It would be nice to talk with someone from Boston again. What's his name?"

"Duncan MacGregor. Most everyone calls him Mac. He's the best neurosurgeon at Harbor Hospital. Did you meet him when you were in my lab?"

"No. We research types didn't have much contact with real doctors."

"Arrange coffee with him and ask him your questions. He's a good guy as well as a great brain surgeon. I'll text you his contact details."

Sophie arranged a meeting with MacGregor a few days after he arrived in Istanbul.

At a cafe beside the Spice Bazaar, they drank Turkish coffee and munched on *baklava*, *tulumba*, and *sigara boregi* while gazing at the Bosphorus. The sun baked everything and everyone as ferries docked and departed, taking commuters to destinations on either the European or Asian shore. The aroma of exotic spices drifted from the open bazaar. Well-fed cats crossed back and forth in the sidewalk in front of them or lazed in the sun.

"Are you here with your family?" Sophie asked.

"Yes—my wife Laura and two children. I've spent a delightful two days being a tourist with them."

"How old are the children? Do they like Istanbul so far?"

"Maggie's thirteen and Peter's eleven. They love it. We've spent time in Hagia Sophia, the Blue Mosque, Grand Bazaar, Topkapi Palace, Archeological Museum, and underground cistern. It's amazing how much history and interest is concentrated in a small area of the old city."

"There's a lot more to see. My favorite is Chora church—I think they call it the Kariye Mosque now. And there's the Roman wall, the bridges of the Bosporus..."

"They're cruising the Bosporus right now, and they'll fly back to Boston in two days."

"And you? When will you go back?" Sophie found it extremely easy to talk to this man, who despite his elevated status as a professor of neurosurgery seemed to be a normal human being.

"I'll see the sights with them for a two days, then focus on the scientific meeting after they return to the USA." He finished his coffee and stared at Sophie. "But tell me why we are meeting. Grace said you had a problem you'd like to discuss."

"Can we walk over to Sirkeci Park?" Sophie asked. "It's one of my favorite places, and it's more private than the cafés on the waterfront." She led Mac to a bench under the broad leaves of a plane tree. A few couples walking in the distance on the quiet paths were the only other pedestrians. The smell of fresh green leaves filled the air, and the sun dappled the ground in front of them.

"I've spent the last eight months setting up the manufacturing sequence for an anti-anxiety dietary supplement called *NoFear*," Sophie said, writing the name on a pad from her purse. "It's made from an ancient Chinese herb and is now being shipped to the US for general distribution."

"Interesting name. How did you get involved with the project?"

"Grace Wu suggested I go to China to study making a commercial product out of herbal medicine after I finished my post-doc with her, and this project came up while I was in Yichang. I wasn't sure about it at first—even went to a traditional herbalist to see what the herb contained."

"And?"

"The herbalist said it was banned because it had too many bad side effects."

"But you decided to go ahead despite that warning?"

Sophie looked around her. "There's more to the story. Just before I got the NoFear project, I lost both my Chinese government grant and my American university position. I got incredibly anxious because I don't have a family and recently suffered a messy divorce. My ex-husband said I was a workaholic, which is probably true."

Her voice faltered, and she looked away for a moment. "I had no job, no income, not even a way to leave the country. I got so anxious and depressed I tried to jump into the Chang Jiang River at Three Gorges Dam. That's the river you probably know as the Yangtze, the most important river in China. I would certainly have died."

"Ouch," Mac said, shaking his head. "I'm glad you didn't succeed. What happened to stop you?"

"A Chinese government official named Jin grabbed my arm and kept me dangling over the waterfall a minute or so to make me realize what I was trying to do. He pulled me back to safety and offered me this project. Given the circumstances it wasn't exactly a choice for me to turn it down. I had to do what he asked or go to jail."

"What do you think's going on?" Mac asked.

"The official seemed to know I had special expertise. I think he wanted to get this material manufactured quickly." She began to cry.

Mac stared. "I'm sure you realize the involvement of someone like Jin makes any decision about backing out a lot more complicated. But what's the problem with the compound you've created?"

"Two problems." Sophie felt the need to stand to lessen the uneasiness rising inside her despite her daily NoFear doses. "First, it may work too well. I've been taking it three times a day and it has eliminated my anxiety, which is what I hoped for. The problem is it also removed fears that warned me of danger. A couple of times I found myself in parts of Istanbul I shouldn't have gone to, and I get the urge to do crazy things like jump in front of a cab to make it stop. The way Istanbul cabbies drive, I could have a very short life." She twisted her hands and began to pace back and forth in front of Mac.

"The main problem is that the compound seems to be addictive," she blurted out, "at least for me. I tried to stop it and had terrible withdrawal symptoms—headaches, nausea. I think I even had a seizure while I was asleep."

"It sounds as though you should get off it, but I would recommend tapering it over several weeks. Is that your question?"

"No, my question is not about me. It's about NoFear itself. What's my responsibility when I know it's a dangerous drug? Should I try to stop it from being manufactured?"

"Could you stop it if you wanted to?"

"I have something in mind. And there's another thing. All our production is presently being shipped to the United States. Why would that be?"

"Maybe because America has the biggest world market in dietary supplements. We spend over fifty billion dollars a year on these untested compounds."

"I suppose, but I'm worried about the effects of this so-called dietary supplement, especially its addictive properties. They could be disastrous in a country like America. I think the whole production of this drug should be stopped."

"Who is financing the project? China? Turkey? Big Pharma? The money trail will lead to the answer about the consequences of stopping its production."

"It's a company called Natural Supplements Inc., but I don't know where their money comes from."

Mac sat back for several seconds. "Based on what you've told me, I agree with you that production of this drug should be stopped or at least paused until further trials can be completed. At minimum it needs some kind of government regulation."

He looked at his watch and scribbled his cell phone number on a business card. "I have to meet my family. I hope you'll be able to work out what to do in your own time and way. Thanks so much for introducing me to this beautiful park. Please feel free to call me any time."

She stared at the card, realizing that this man was not only a practicing neurosurgeon but a full professor at the most prestigious medical school in the world. "Thank you, Professor MacGregor," she said as he left. "I know what I'm going to have to do."

不怕

CHAPTER SIX

SOPHIE MEETS JIN

GALATA TOWER PLAZA, ISTANBUL

Two days later, Sophie sipped Turkish coffee in the plaza beside Istanbul's Galata Tower waiting for her Chinese contact Jin. She listened to muezzins calling the faithful to prayer, smelled the fragrance of cardamom and other spices, and felt engulfed by the ceaseless foot, bicycle, and motor traffic around her.

Jin showed up half an hour late. "Why did you insist on this meeting?" he asked, leaning across the bistro table toward Sophie. "The manufacturing facility for NoFear is running, distribution to the United States has begun, and you're getting a regular paycheck. What's the problem? And why a meeting in person rather than on Zoom? It's not an easy trip from Beijing to Istanbul."

Sophie stared at the sludge left from her coffee and tried to block out the street vendors, children, cats, and tourists swarming in the space around them. She wondered who Jin's superiors were, what they were doing with NoFear production, how he had learned to speak English so well.

Although it had been eight months since Three Gorges, she still knew nothing about him. Even with NoFear in her system, she was worried she would not be able to guide this discussion to its unwelcome conclusion.

She took a deep breath. "You know how helpful NoFear has been for me," she began. "I was suicidal before I took it, overcome with anxiety." She stood and began circling the table, unable to contain the energy building within her. "In the past months, I've lost my anxiety and accomplished amazing things. I synthesized the active ingredient from the *Bupa* plant, made a pill out of it, and oversaw the first shipments headed for America. I didn't need sleep, food, or companions. I worked without pause."

"Of course." Jin said. "What's your point?"

"About a month after I started to take my magic pills, I developed an urge to do stupid dangerous things. Shoplift from a lingerie store just for the thrill of it. Walk in front of a car just to watch the driver slam his brakes on and shake his fist. Wonder what would happen if I jumped from this tower." She pointed to the Galata Tower observation platform fifty-one meters above them. "I spend a lot of my time now stopping an urge to get in harm's way, and I don't like it."

She stepped from the café plaza into the street, blocking a cyclist who swerved wildly and cursed at her as he careened off course.

She laughed at him and flexed her elbow at his stream of abuse. "See what I mean?"

"I cannot help it if you use the benefits of this substance foolishly," Jin said.

"Ah, but if I'm fighting the urge to live dangerously all the time, won't that happen to anyone using NoFear? Everyone taking it will want to do dangerous things just to keep stimulated. Can you imagine thousands of users testing the limits of the law every day?"

She saw a shadow cross Jin's face, perhaps a recognition that she had discovered too much. "That is not our concern," he said.

"It should be. And here's another problem. In college I read about rats that had electrodes implanted into their brain. When they pressed a lever, they got pleasure. After a few weeks they died while still pressing the lever."

"So what?"

"Since I've arrived in Istanbul, I have no friends and no interest in food or drink. NoFear had made me into a fearless rat. I tried to stop it for two days and had withdrawal symptoms of the worst kind. Headaches, abdominal pain, nausea, tremors. I've seen friends go through opiate or alcohol withdrawal with less trouble."

She leaned on the table and stared into her companion's hard black eyes "Your dietary supplement is both dangerous and addictive."

Jin jumped up and grabbed her collar to pull her face within a few centimeters of his. He hissed with a whisper that chilled her to the marrow, "Your puny experience is of no interest to me. Is this the reason you brought me halfway across the world?"

"No," Sophie spat out. "I want the production of NoFear to stop. Now let me go or I'll call the police."

Jin stood back.

"Stopping production is impossible," he hissed.

"Why?"

"You are not entitled to know the answer to that question."

"Then I want out."

Jin narrowed his eyelids. "What do you mean?"

"I don't want to be part of the manufacturing process."

Jin laughed, then pulled out a stiletto knife and laid it on the table. He whispered, "Do you see this blade? You have no idea about the people you are dealing with. If you try to separate yourself from us. I will personally slit your throat."

Sophie stared at the weapon. "This is Istanbul. You can't just pull a knife and—"

"Look around you. Do you see anybody who would rush to help? Even if I killed you right here, your death would be seen as an unfortunate incident and no one would give a damn. Doctor Grainger, it is best for you to crawl back into your hole and do exactly what I say."

Jin slipped the knife back into his jacket pocket and began to walk away. Sophie, trembling with anger, shouted after him, "We'll put children's lives in danger."

He turned back and took a step toward her. Despite the NoFear circulating in her blood, her heart thumped in her chest. "That is their option," Jin said. "Freedom of choice is the foundation of your whole American system, isn't it? By allowing people to have NoFear, we are simply promoting freedom."

He disappeared into the crowd heading back to Taksim square.

Sophie stood, heart pounding but teeth clenched and eyelids narrowed. Soon Jin would know what free will looked like in action.

不怕

CHAPTER SEVEN

THE BOSPORUS SWIMMER

LACIVERT RESTAURANT, ISTANBUL

A swimmer? At this hour? In the middle of the Bosporus? Duncan MacGregor directed his binoculars over the surface of the moonlit waves to find the bobbing head again. With his family back in Boston and his neurosurgical conference almost over, he was dining at the famed Lacivert fish restaurant on the Asian side of the Bosporus. Using the binoculars provided by the restaurant to scan the waterway, he saw what he thought was a night bather.

He beckoned to his waiter. "Could I be seeing a swimmer in the Bosporus at this hour?"

"No. Is forbidden."

"I'm sure I see someone swimming. Look for yourself."

Mac handed the binoculars to the server, who took a cursory glance and returned them with the reply, "I see nothing. And we provide these to look at ships, not people."

Mac swept the water's surface again. In the bright pathway reflecting the moon, he saw a pale face and dark hair, with the flash of arms. "Look. There! Near the bridge. Halfway across." He pointed towards the center of the choppy channel.

The waiter crouched with the field glasses and this time followed the line of Mac's arm. "You are right. I see now," the waiter said. "Crazy. Ship will run him down or current will sweep him out to sea." He shook his head.

The conversations of fellow diners and aromas of food faded for Mac as the conviction of an impending tragedy gripped him. He sprang to his feet and his pulse raced as he pictured an exhausted swimmer drowning. "Is the water taxi at the dock on this side?"

"Yes, but it's only to take guests back and forth to the European side. It's the Bosporus police patrol's job to—"

Mac was already heading for the restaurant's dock, where the helmsman leaned against the gunwale of the water taxi smoking a Turkish cigarette. "I need your help," Mac said. "Can you get me to the center of the channel?"

"My job is only to transport restaurant customers to the other side."

"I'm a restaurant customer. And that's where I'm going. Just not all the way." Mac tried to hide his rising temper and continued with what he hoped was a conciliatory tone. "Look, I saw a swimmer in the middle of the channel. If a freighter doesn't kill him, the current will."

"I only take orders from restaurant owner."

Mac could feel a flush begin in his neck. He looked to the night sky, counted a dozen stars, and turned back toward the driver. "I'll buy you a carton of cigarettes." He sniffed the foul smoke rising into the sky. "As long as you don't smoke them until I'm gone."

The Turk paused, shrugged, ground out his smoke, and climbed into the small boat. Mac followed him, sitting on the leather cushions along the side seats as the motor roared into life. The sound shattered the nocturnal quiet and the smell of motor oil replaced the cool freshness of the night breeze. The small craft bobbed and rolled in the choppy sea, unsettling Mac's recently satiated stomach.

"Do you have a searchlight?" Mac asked, trying to turn his attention away from his gastrointestinal system, desperate to track down the swimmer he had spotted.

The captain flipped on the mercury beam mounted on the cabin roof, creating a circle of light on the whitecaps. He swept the bright beam back and forth in front of the small boat as it moved forward.

He gestured to a covered equipment box at the side of the cabin. Mac rifled through it and retrieved a flashlight, playing it over the dark surfaces beside and behind the boat.

In the distance, the European side of Istanbul glowed faintly. The first bridge cast a dim multicolored glow above them. An ocean freighter slid in front of them as it travelled from the Sea of Marmara to the Black Sea.

So beautiful, so deadly...

Mac swept his light in wide arcs, realized his weak beam was inadequate for the job, but felt obligated to do something. The captain headed with the current, propelled by the power of wind and wave. After a few minutes he grunted and pointed far downstream, where the searchlight illuminated a pale patch in the water. Seconds later, they slowed beside a human form floating face down, bobbing with the current.

Using a grappling hook, Mac hauled the body onto the floor of the boat. A boy about seventeen, wearing pants but no shirt or shoes. Flaccid limbs, blue lips, closed eyelids, extremities dead white. No carotid pulse, no respiratory efforts. When Mac forced the eyelids open and shone the flashlight into them, no response from the dilated pupils.

Mac shuddered. These were all signs of death.

Moving more by reflex than hope, Mac rolled the teenager three quarters prone and slapped him on the back to eject water from the lungs. He found none. Wondering briefly why there was no water if the boy had drowned, he turned the body back to a supine position and began chest compressions.

"Head for the landing site and call an ambulance!" he shouted to the skipper, who had already redirected the boat toward the European side of the Bosporus. Even with the engines straining at full throttle, they made slow progress against the powerful current. By the time they reached the shore, the engines seemed exhausted.

Mac's felt despair as he realized the boy had not responded to his resuscitation efforts.

Flashing lights of EMT and police vehicles illuminated the landing. The emergency techs, waiting at the dock, slid a spine board under the victim and lifted him onto a stretcher. A woman in police uniform stepped forward and introduced herself as Sergeant Handan Borlak. "What happened?" she asked, glancing briefly at the business card Mac handed her.

"I saw the boy swimming while I was dining at the Lacivert restaurant on the Asian side. I commandeered the launch to rescue him, but he was pulseless when I dragged him out of the water."

"Why are you in Istanbul, Dr. MacGregor?"

"I'm a neurosurgeon attending a meeting of the World Federation of Neurosurgery. My home is in Boston. That's in the United States."

Borlak smiled a little. "I'm a Red Sox fan. The world is smaller than you think. Where are you staying?"

"The Hilton near Taksim."

One of the EMT techs signaled to Borlak, who walked

away and listened to a few brief sentences in Turkish.

"The boy has been declared dead," she said, returning to Mac. "We'll have to ask you to file an official report. How long will you be here?"

"The conference ends in two days."

"Please meet me at the police station in Taksim tomorrow afternoon at three o'clock."

"Do you know anything about the victim?" Mac asked.

"His friends here had a lot to say." She pointed to a cluster of young men and women jabbing at their smartphones. "Claim he just decided he should swim across to the other side of the Bosporus and dove in before they could stop him."

A young woman with large eyes flicked a strand of jet-black hair from her face as she approached Mac and Borlak. "Excuse me, are you Dr. Duncan McGregor?" she asked.

"I am," Mac said as he shook the woman's hand. "And you are?"

"Sedar Selcuk. I'm a medical student at Medical Park University. My dad's a neurosurgeon here in Istanbul. You and I met about three years ago at a convention in London."

"Nice to see you again," Mac said, remembering the encounter only vaguely.

Borlak motioned Mac to join her as she moved Sedar and her friends to the corner of the dock. "What do you know about this boy?" Borlak asked.

"His name is Hassan. We celebrated his birthday in Belek and chose the shore route to go home. When he got to this dock, he ordered the driver to stop. He got out and started gushing about how beautiful the bridge looked and how the moon made like a pathway on the water."

"Did you do any drugs before this?" Borlak was apparently not one to mince her words.

"Gosh no," Sedar said. "We don't want to end up in jail."

"So go on about Hassan," Borlak said.

"He got more and more excited about how inviting the Bosporus looked in the moonlight, and how he had missed the Cross-the-Bosporus swim this year."

"And?"

"He kicked his shoes off, ripped off his jacket, and dove into the water."

"Did he say anything?"

"We think he shouted *Korku yok*.

"Which means?" Mac asked.

"No fear," Sedar said.

不怕

CHAPTER EIGHT

POLIS

TAKSIM POLICE STATION, ISTANBUL

Korku yok.
No fear.

Mac couldn't get the words out of his head. NoFear was the drug Sophie Grainger was working on, the one that she thought was too dangerous to market.

Did those words summarize the cause of Hassan's death? Why did the boy shout them? A battle cry? A claim to invincibility? Did he think he could safely swim the Bosporus alone at night because NoFear had taken away his common sense?

During the day, the event churned in his mind with turbulence as great as the restless Bosporus. Hassan's limp body interrupted his conference attention. The boy's blue lips and sightless eyes invaded his dreams, startling him awake.

He analyzed the events like a surgical case, trying to dissect what went wrong. What if he had used the binoculars twenty minutes earlier? Could he have been more vigorous in his resuscitation? How could he have kept the boy from drowning?

In the afternoon, he walked the few blocks to Taksim square to meet with Sergeant Borlak. Traffic clogged

Cumhuriyet Caddesi, with yellow taxis competing with waves of subway commuters for access to the streets. The esplanade in the middle of the road created a double hazard for the unwary driver, with heedless businesspeople and joggers and shoe-shine artists crossing everywhere.

The police station, an inconspicuous townhouse with a Turkish flag and POLIS printed on the window, hid on a back street beside the square. Mac had difficulty finding it, despite his smartphone GPS, and arrived a few minutes late.

As he swung the door of the station open, the odor of sweat and musty rugs made him take a step back. Twenty men and women occupied a space slightly bigger than his living room at home. Some sat on folding chairs, but the majority leaned against the peeling paint of the wall. The rug was grimy, the space was lit by fluorescent lights, and sunlight barely passed through dirt-streaked windows.

At the end of the room, a uniformed officer sat in a plastic booth that protected him on three sides. Beside him, a closed door with an X on it appeared to provide access to the back rooms of the station.

"I have an appointment with Sergeant Borlak," Mac said as he approached the desk.

"No English," the man said, lifting his head in a gesture of negativity.

"Borlak. Sergeant Borlak."

The man shrugged, then pointed to the waiting room. "Wait."

"But I am already late for my appointment."

The policeman released a stream of Turkish invective that sounded like the product of a miserable shift. At the end of the tirade, the man stood up and pointed to the far corner, shouting in heavily accented English, "There."

Mac knew horror stories of arrest and detention in Turkish prisons with no provocation. He headed for the corner.

A familiar voice interrupted him. "Dr. MacGregor. Over here."

Mac turned back to see Borlak calling from the previously closed doorway.

He moved toward her. "My apologies. Not so easy to find the station if you aren't a native."

"No problem," Borlak replied. "My assistant will take your statement, but I have a special request first. Hassan's parents would like to meet you. And there's an autopsy finding you should know before you talk with them."

"The situation seems simple. The boy tried to swim against a deadly current and drowned."

"Except for one small detail," she said. "His breathing and heartbeat stopped while he was swimming. Drowning was not the cause of death."

"But he looked as though he had just drowned when I saw him."

"There was almost no water in the lungs, so our pathologist is certain drowning was not the cause of death. She's signing it out as a cardiorespiratory arrest of unknown cause. And that means there's nothing you could have done to help him."

Mac felt relief but also concern. "Why would he have a cardiac arrest? Was he on drugs? Did you do a tox screen?"

"Of course. That's where it becomes interesting. His blood had a chemical thus far unknown to us. Perhaps that made him push his heart beyond its limits."

"A drug so powerful it would lead a teenager to drive his heart to cardiac arrest?" Mac asked. "Our body usually has safeguards to prevent us from exerting ourselves that much. No drug I know reduces fear or has any other effect so much you swim yourself to death."

"Apparently this is one such compound. We're using mass spectroscopy to analyze its structure now. Are you ready to meet his parents?"

She led Mac into a small bare room with a table and several chairs. A short auburn-haired woman sat holding hands with a man with a mustache and grey hair. Tears streaked the woman's makeup. A video camera monitored the table from one ceiling corner; its red light shone steadily. The only illumination came from buzzing fluorescent tubes.

"This is Dr. MacGregor," Sergeant Borlak said, "the American neurosurgeon who tried to save Hassan."

Hassan's father rose to his feet and extended a hand to Mac. His wife remained in her chair, wiping tears from her face.

"I'm so sorry about your son," Mac said.

"Thank you for help him," Hassan's mother said. "A good boy. Why he tried that swim?" She sobbed and her husband sat back down beside her, wrapping his arm around her shoulders.

"I have no idea," Mac said. "Was he a good swimmer?"

"Excellent when small boy," she stammered, "but last few years he never swim. He afraid of fish, water germs, darkness, everything."

"Then why would he even be near the water at night?" Mac asked.

"We start to have hope," Hassan's father said. "We found new medication to help him. He was getting better, start to go out, have friends again..."

"Medication was called *NoFear—Korku yok*. Seemed to be life changing for our boy," Hassan's mother said, looking through tears at her husband, who nodded and pressed her hand. "We learn about from Tik Tok online."

"And it helped?" Mac tried not to let his distress show. Online medications were unpredictable in composition and sometimes much more dangerous than they seemed.

"A miracle," Hassan's mother said. "He could go to school again. Birthday came and he went out yesterday. Then we find out he died."

Her husband interrupted her. "Doctor, something we not understand. Sergeant Borlak says Hassan died before drowned. How is that possible?" He stared at Borlak, who remained silent.

"Look," Hassan's mother said, "Turkish doctors good, but need proof everything is done to understand why our son die. You help us?"

"I'm only here at a conference. I'm going back to Boston in three days."

"Can you help for those days?" the mother asked.

"The police are good here. They don't need help." Mac looked at Borlak, who shrugged.

"Dr. MacGregor, you have child?" The father's tone was challenging and pleading at the same time.

Mac nodded.

"Can you imagine swimming to death?"

"No," Mac said, thinking about his son and the overwhelming devastation he would feel if Peter died. "I'll stay until we know more about how Hassan died," he said to Hassan's parents.

不怕

CHAPTER NINE

SOPHIE'S DECISION

ISTANBUL, TÜRKIYE

After her disastrous meeting with Jin, Sophie decided that the only way to stop NoFear production would be to remove its manufacturing facility. She would destroy the equipment she had developed so carefully, set fire to the lab as an extra precaution, and escape to Romania by boat while Istanbul's authorities were dealing with the flames. She had arranged a job to teach English as a second language in a private school in Constanta, a Romanian city on the Black Sea. The school asked no questions about her background. It seemed clear to them she spoke English perfectly.

She had already leased a boat for her escape. Built for speed and comfort, it boasted a composite construction both strong and buoyant.

News of Hassan's death in the local newspaper put her plan into action. The press would soon uncover the fact that Hassan was taking NoFear and would trace its manufacture to this facility. She knew the building security guard napped from two to three a.m., making that her hour for action.

She spent her day packing a bag of clothing, sequestering her passport, wallet, and phone in a waterproof container, and buying a can of gasoline to stoke the fire. At nine p.m.

she motored to the dock in front of the factory building and secured her vessel to it.

"You can't keep a boat here overnight," a voice bellowed in Turkish from a harbor police cruiser ten meters off the shore.

Was her plan going to be destroyed by a parking violation? "I'm delivering a package to an office in the Old Port Building," she shouted.

"Which office?"

Sophie gave the name of an office across from her and held her breath. *Weird*, she thought, *I'm really not afraid.* One way or another she would have to make them go away.

The police cruiser paused, then turned around and disappeared.

Sophie left the dock and walked back to her apartment, where she set the alarm for two a.m. and napped despite the excitement rising within her.

Awakened by the shrill signal, she returned to the dock and watched from the shadows as the guard made his rounds and headed for his nap.

With her face covered by a dark hoodie and the gasoline can in her left hand, she sprayed her building's CCTV cameras with black paint, turned off the water supply, and cut the security alarm cables. She headed for a door with glass panels at the rear of the building, wrapped her hoodie around her hand, broke a panel, and reached through the opening to unlock the door. No alarm sounded. Once inside, she felt her way to her own office and repeated the maneuver.

Sophie now had forty-five minutes to destroy the pharma facility she had helped to create. Climbing onto a chair, she disabled the smoke alarms, then took an axe from the fire emergency case in the hallway. She smashed the first piece of equipment, spewing electronic components in every direction, then repeated her attack on four more sophisticated units. NoFear-pill production at this facility was over, but just to be sure...

She sprinkled gasoline over the floor and threw in a match. The flame almost exploded, licking at the wooden supports for the machinery, roaring with increasing fury as she bolted out the door.

She raced down the back stairs that emptied into an alley normally used for trash storage. Restricted by high brick walls on each side, the passageway had only occasional incandescent bulbs lighting its boundaries. Several cats scurried from garbage bag to garbage bag along her path. The passage ended on the waterfront. After confirming that no one was patrolling the area, she ran across the dock to her boat.

Small and powerful, with a range of 400 kilometers on one tank of gas, the black vessel was almost invisible in the dim moonlight. The engines roared to life as she maneuvered it into the center of the Bosporus channel.

At full throttle in a calm sea, her escape yacht could make thirty-one knots. Driving against the surging current, she made fewer than twenty. She stayed at the periphery of the freighter lanes, where container ships felt their way along the dark passage guided by pilots from the Turkish authority.

Only when she was at the first bridge over the Bosporus did she look back, spotting distant smoke rising into the sky. Covered by the clouds of night, she sped under the bridge.

The shore lights that she knew belonged to hotels and private homes gave way to longer and longer patches of trees. Past the Naval Academy, past the remnant of the old wall of Istanbul, under the second bridge, she continued steadily north. The engine whine became a reassuring drone. Gulls squawked, muezzins chanted from mosque towers, freighters signaled their passage, in what was now early morning. The air flew by cold and fresh. Spray dotted the windscreen of the yacht.

She felt ready for her new life by the time she reached the junction of the Bosporus with the Black Sea. Her boat entered the open expanse of water with the muscles of a stallion. Freed from the Bosporus current, its roar quieted to a hum.

Sophie relaxed as the destruction of her laboratory became more distant. The coast melted away. No other ships dotted the sea. The chop of the hull against light waves provided a counterpoint to the screech of gulls. As a chill breeze splayed her long black hair around her face, she closed the cockpit cover and drove on.

She set the GPS autopilot to maintain course and let her eyelids close.

A turbulent sea startled her awake. Black clouds darkened the sky as torrential rain lashed against the fiberglass canopy over the control room.

The boat rolled and twisted in the gathering swells. Sophie wrenched the wheel to keep the bow slicing into the waves, cresting with one and diving into the trough of the next. The motion made her violently ill—no human vestibular system was designed to withstand that kind of tossing. She felt a burn in her throat as her stomach regurgitated its acid. She retched over and over, grateful that she had no food to vomit.

The wind whipped the surface of the sea into a frenzy, building seven-foot waves against the rain-soaked sky.

Darkness descended further, and her world became a maelstrom of swirling, violent, pounding water.

She knew about these squalls. They descend from a cloudless sky, roiling the ocean surface with power deadly enough to stop all shipping until they passed. Even massive container ships feared breaking up with their overwhelming force.

She fought with the wheel now, the boat wanting to slide into troughs of turbulence, to roll with the waves rather than into them. It pitched and yawed like a plaything in the hands of an ancient god. She decided to keep the throttle full with the idea of cresting the waves, but the swells, now reaching ten feet, could sometimes not be mounted. She smashed through them with the hull screaming in pain, every ounce of tensile strength in its construction trying to avoid breakup.

In darkness still, with GPS navigation lost and running lights penetrating nothing, she felt her ship being driven toward the eastern side of the Black Sea. This was not the direction she wished. The hurricane force winds pounded her small craft without pause. The hull creaked and groaned, sending shivers into the cockpit. The steering wheel was no longer her locus of control. It was the only thing she could hold onto. Afraid she might drown if the boat foundered, she loosened her seat belt and yanked at a life preserver, trying to put it on while still managing the wheel.

Blinding lighting followed by deafening thunder took away all thought. She screamed in terror. For a moment, she was again a five-year old child hiding under the bed until the storm stopped.

Except there was no bed, and this was not just a thunderstorm.

She threw out the sea anchor and let it play out. After

that, she could only hold on. The wheel spun as the boat came broadside into a huge wave that broke over her like a waterfall. She felt herself rolling, upside down, then right again.

She looked up to face a wave larger than she had ever seen. Cresting higher than twenty feet, it would smash the boat into small fragments if it broke with the vessel broadside.

With all her strength she twisted the wheel around to bring the bow into the oncoming disaster. The ship hesitated, then climbed toward the wall of water rushing toward it. The engine stalled, sputtered, caught again. The bow lifted, gradually headed upward almost at a seventy-five-degree angle. She held her breath. *Would it be able to ride the wave?*

It inched toward the crest, engine screaming and hull quivering with effort. Her hands were so painful she had to release the wheel. The boat crawled into a backward flip, toppled by the strength of immeasurable tons of water. The bow reared up in front of her and Sophie dashed against the cockpit top, side, bottom. She shot her arms out to find something to hold onto. Nothing.

No screaming this time; just terror.

The storm abated as quickly as it had come. Sophie had no idea what time it was. Her smartwatch had lost battery power and presented only a blank dial.

Dawn spread with dazzling radiance. It made waves sparkle and the rocky coastline appear from the early morning darkness like a sleeping giant.

Sophie rose tentatively to her feet, testing and inspecting her battered frame. Bruises, small lacerations, tears in her clothes. Chest and shoulders sore where she must have smashed against the life-saving harness lashing her to the seat early in the storm. A terrible headache. Nothing broken. Left leg the worst: numb, compressed between the captain's chair and steering wheel. The leg began to tingle as she released it, burning with sensory fire. Although she knew this was just the first phase of recovery from nerve compression, it hurt like crazy.

Her head throbbed. She explored the scalp where it hurt most, felt a tender lump under a mess of matted hair, and drew her fingers back to inspect them. Streaked with blood, but no active bleeding.

"Rather a mess, Ms. Grainger," she muttered to herself, "but not a disaster." Her lips were dry and crusted and her voice croaked. The boat bobbed in the still air. A few seagull cries punctuated the gentle lapping of the sea. Otherwise, nothing but water, wind, and sun around her.

Wincing, she pulled herself above the gunwale. The windscreen had been shattered and the wheel handled erratically, suggesting a glitch in the steering cables. She could get no radio transmission or GPS signal.

She slid the cabin door open and descended below deck. The sump pump chugged under moist floorboards. There was water in the bilge and a dank smell permeated the small space.

The boat's head was intact and she used it, grateful for small mercies.

Back on deck, Sophie retrieved her cell phone from its waterproof pack and identified the nearest port—Zonguldak, a Turkish town on the Black Sea shore. She aimed her fractured ship toward the town as the coastline appeared, silhouetted against the morning sky.

With a start, she realized the shore was coming closer. Fast. A current so strong and swift it could not be resisted.

She stared helplessly at the rocky coast ahead as the current increased. Her heart raced and she wiped sweat from her brow, but she could do nothing. She considered whether to jump and decided it would be better to stay with the boat.

Moments later she felt the shuddering of her boat breaking up on shoals. Thrown against the bulwark, she hit her head with a savageness that made it spin. Everything faded to black.

不怕

CHAPTER TEN

SOPHIE'S EXIT

ZONGULDAK, TÜRKIYE

Sophie tried to make her eyes focus. Everything around her seemed blurry, confused. She couldn't remember where she was or how she got here. She had a terrible headache.

She scanned the room through half-closed eyes. Her bed was the only one in the room. A dilapidated armchair sat with her clothes piled on it in the corner. Portraits of former and current Turkish presidents hung on painted plaster walls. Light filtered through a small dirty window. The walls were otherwise empty.

A hospital. She stared at an IV in her left arm and a bottle of saline hanging above it, a johnny tied loosely at the back. No monitors. A cord she could pull, but no response when she pulled it.

She closed her eyes, trying to relieve herself of her excruciating headache, and lay back against the pillow. Eventually, a nurse appeared.

"You're awake," the nurse said, eyebrows raised.

"Where am I?" Sophie asked.

"Zonguldak Devlet Hastanesi," the nurse said, "and I apologize for English. I one of few nurses who speaks it."

"What happened to me?" Sophie asked. "How did I get here?"

"Wrecked boat. Ambulance. Unconscious since then three hours. Breathing and vital signs OK."

"How do I get out of here?"

The nurse shook her head. "You must rest. Have family?"

"No, no one."

"We found phone and charged it. Maybe call friends." She handed Sophie her charged cell phone, waiting a few moments for Sophie's response."

"Thank you," Sophie said, picking up the phone and unlocking it.

"I come back later," the nurse said and left.

Fighting her headache and with eyesight sometimes blurring, Sophie began to scroll through her contact list, stopping every few lines. She realized she had no friends she wanted to call. She paused at Dr. Duncan MacGregor, the most recent addition to her contacts. Perhaps a neurosurgeon would be helpful in this situation.

She called Mac, who answered on the second ring.

"Dr. MacGregor, this is Sophie Grainger," she began. "We had coffee earlier this week. I've had a boat accident. I'm in a hospital in Zonguldak. Is there any way you can—

"Zonguldak?" Mac asked, his voice showing concern. "Where is that?"

"On the Black Sea." Sophie said.

"What happened?" Mac asked.

"The nurse told me I crashed my boat last night."

"How does your head feel?"

"I've got a splitting headache and have trouble thinking straight."

"OK. I'm going to rent a car and get up to see you as soon as possible. Meanwhile, can you ask the doctor to get a CT scan?" He hung up.

Sophie rang the bell, but no one came. When the nurse finally reappeared, Sophie asked "How do I get a CT scan?"

"Should speak with doctor," the nurse said.

Sophie drifted off to sleep despite her headache. Troubled by nightmares, she awoke two hours later to find Jin standing beside her bed.

"Jin! What are you doing here? How did you get in?" she asked. Her heart started to pound as badly as her head, and she found it hard to think. She pulled the covers around her and surveyed the room for an escape route.

"This is not a secure facility," Jin said.

"How did you find me?" she asked.

"We put GPS software on your phone. I've stayed around in Istanbul since we met. I heard about the plant on the news and was searching for you until the phone suddenly started to give a signal four hours ago."

He took a syringe out of his pocket. "You were stupid to have destroyed our manufacturing facility, Sophie."

"Wasn't me."

"Of course it was. You were the only one with access, and here you are after an attempt to escape. Why did you do it?"

She was too exhausted to continue her lie. "It was the only way I could stop NoFear production."

"You didn't stop it. We have other facilities in Asia and Europe you know nothing about. We could hardly supply the demand with this facility alone."

He moved toward the intravenous tubing and injected a syringe full of material into it. "This should make you feel a lot better," he said with merciless eyes focused on her.

"No," Sophie cried, suddenly realizing something was wrong as the material burned in her vein. She pulled at her IV to remove it.

"Too late," Jin said, and left the room. "Goodbye, Sophie Grainger."

Mac arrived two hours later and asked for an American woman named Grainger who had been brought in after a boating accident. Extensive searching through logs and admission sheets finally found Sophie. As he entered the ward, he inquired about her condition at the nursing desk and was told in halting English she was sleeping comfortably.

As soon as he entered her room, he realized she was dead. She lay motionless on two pillows, not breathing. Her face was the color of the sheets surrounding her and her skin was cool to the touch. Her pupils were fixed and widely dilated. She had no pulse.

He began chest compressions and shouted for help. In a few minutes, he was surrounded by nurses and the physician in charge of the ward.

"Are you a relative?" the physician asked.

"No, a friend."

"Stop CPR" the ward doctor said, looming over Mac. "This sort of thing happens all the time. It's a delayed cardiac arrest from the stress and trauma of the accident. No way we can bring her back."

Mac stopped his compressions and stepped back from the lifeless form on the bed. "Will you do a post-mortem to be sure you're right?" he asked.

"We don't have the resources to do an autopsy on everyone who gets admitted after an accident. Besides, the woman has no family. I have made the diagnosis. This is a post-traumatic cardiac arrest. End of story."

"Will you at least check for drugs in her blood?"

"Not necessary. I told you the diagnosis is made."

"But—" Mac said.

"The matter is settled. If you will excuse me, I have living patients to attend to."

不怕

CHAPTER ELEVEN

AUTOPSY

ZONGULDAK, TÜRKIYE

What would have killed Sophie three hours after she had talked with me?

Mac had to find the answer, and that would need an autopsy. He moved to the hospital lobby and called Jim Brogan, a friend who had joined him in several past adventures. Brogan headed the section for terrorism analysis at the CIA and had connections with law enforcement officials around the world. He was the only person Mac knew who might be able to force an autopsy in a foreign country.

Mac checked his watch. One-thirty p.m. in Turkey, six-thirty a.m. in Maryland.

He called despite the early hour.

Brogan answered on the third ring, but his voice had an abrasive edge. "Mac, I hope this is important. I'm just getting ready to leave for work."

"Have you ever heard of a compound called NoFear?" Mac asked.

Brogan remained silent for several seconds, seconds that seemed exceptionally long. "Why?"

"I'm in Turkey, and the name has come up twice in the last three days. A young man taking it drowned in front of me in the Bosporus, and a woman involved in its production just died suddenly in the hospital after a boat accident."

"When are you getting back to the States?"

"A couple of days."

"We should spend some time going over what I know. I'm due to come up to Boston in a week. Perhaps we could meet then. Is that all you wanted me for?"

"No. Right now I need to get an autopsy and drug screen on the woman I just told you about who died early this afternoon. She's an American expat and may have been involved with the Chinese government in some way. The physicians here refuse both autopsy and toxicology."

"What's her name. What hospital?"

"Sophie Grainger. In Zonguldak."

"You're going to have to spell that out for me. I'm not sure I can help."

Mac obliged.

"Give me half an hour" Brogan said, "but I can't promise anything. That's not one of the cities we deal with regularly."

Mac sat in the hospital lobby observing a stream of desperate patients and families that seemed never-ending. It felt to him as if several hours had passed before Brogan called him back. When he checked his watch, it had been forty minutes.

"I've talked to the head of the Zonguldak police prefecture" Brogan said. "He was willing to tag Sophie as a person whose death was of interest. He called the hospital administrator to demand an autopsy. I had a tough time convincing him at first, but it's not often Americans die in their hospital. Not only that, but apparently this woman may be implicated in a fire in Istanbul. The authorities want to find out what's going on as much as we do."

"Thank you, Jim." Mac said. "I owe you one."

"A big one," Brogan said. "Remember, we meet as soon as you get back."

An hour later Mac sat on a stool in the morgue of the Zonguldak hospital. The pathologist, a heavy-set man with a large mustache, dictated the autopsy findings into a microphone as he worked. He spoke mainly Turkish, but occasionally interspersed comments in heavily accented English. "Facial and body contusions compatible with boat smash," he noted to start.

Using a large scalpel, he cut into Sophie's chest and abdomen with a Y-shaped incision extending from each shoulder to the pelvis. Only a trickle of blood accompanied the wounds as the lifeless tissue separated. Flaying the skin and muscle off the chest wall, he next peeled it up over Sophie's face. A screeching saw tore through the ribs and sternum, sending a plume of bone dust into the air. The acrid odor of burning tissue from the heat of the sawblade reached Mac's nostrils despite the mask.

Lifting the bony chest wall like a trap door, the pathologist exposed the heart and lungs and incised the pericardium. "No sign of thrombi or atherosclerotic occlusion," he said as he cut through the coronary arteries. Palpating the lungs, he added, "And no lung infarcts suggesting pulmonary embolism."

"Could I hold on to a vial of blood in case further analysis is needed?" Mac asked.

"Do not mention this to anyone," the pathologist said as he drew a syringe of dark blood from Sophie's heart and handed it to Mac.

"Thank you," Mac said and slipped it into his jacket pocket.

"What about the coronary arteries?" he asked, knowing that sometimes a blocked artery can cause sudden death even if signs of infarction have not had time to appear.

A slice through the artery wall revealed nothing but dark blood dripping out of the vessel. "No clots," the pathologist said. He ran the bowel, palpated the pancreas, examined the kidneys, opened the bladder. "Nothing here to explain death," he added.

"Now the brain," the pathologist said, poising his knife for the next attack. "We should at least be able to exclude a hemorrhage as the cause of death." He made a circular incision around the scalp and drilled several large holes in the bone, then used a saw to remove most of the skull. It became a bony bowl as big as his two hands.

Mac could not help thinking how different this was from the meticulous technique a neurosurgeon uses when exposing the brain.

"No sign of epidural clot," the pathologist said, displaying the smooth surface of the brain lining. "Now check for a possible subdural." He sliced through the dura. "No subdural or intracerebral hemorrhage either. And no brain swelling of the type that suggests a massive stroke."

He put his scalpel down, wiped his gloved hands on his apron, and turned to Mac. "Doctor Duncan, we found no cause of death here. If you need get back to Istanbul, please go ahead. I finish up details."

"Thank you for doing the autopsy so promptly." Mac felt a queasiness in his gut precisely because the autopsy gave no answer. The blood specimen might add valuable information if he could get it through customs and safely into the hands of his colleague Grace Wu in Boston, but that was a big if.

He headed back to Istanbul with the vial nestled in his shirt pocket. En route, he called Brogan. "We finished the postmortem on Sophie Grainger. No obvious cause of death."

"That worries me," Brogan said.

"I did get a vial of serum to analyze in Boston. That may tell us more."

"Great work," Brogan said. "I've been looking into the story you told. Let me give you an idea of what we're dealing with. Sophie Grainger was involved in the manufacture of NoFear, a compound derived from the Chinese *Bupa* plant. Remarkably effective anti-anxiety agent."

"I know. She talked about it when we had coffee. Said it helped her own anxiety but had some bad side effects."

"One thing that happens, whether it's a side effect or not, is that people do stupid things when they're taking it," Brogan said.

"Like trying to swim the Bosporus at night, or burning down your manufacturing facility?" Mac asked.

"Yes, and the worrisome part is that our intel suggests the Chinese government is distributing this drug mainly in the United States. It smells like they're using it as a bioweapon to disrupt all our systems. They may have bought some lobbyists and congress representatives to keep anyone from investigating it. They're pushing its distribution hard. Endorsements are all over Tik Tok. Perhaps they think enough events where people take crazy risks will destabilize our government."

"That makes perfect sense with what she told me," Mac said. "A Chinese official coerced her to manufacture the drug, saying she would otherwise go to jail. Do you think she was killed because she tried to stop NoFear production in some way?"

"It's possible," Brogan said. "Blood toxicology should tell the story. You were right to demand the autopsy, as usual. Sorry about my attitude when you did."

不怕

CHAPTER TWELVE

LEAVING TÜRKIYE

ISTANBUL, TÜRKIYE

A police officer was waiting in the lobby of the Hilton when Mac returned to Istanbul.

"Sergeant Borlak wanted us to take you to meet with her as soon as you got back to the hotel. Will you come with us, please?"

Mac entered the police van and sat quietly as it headed toward the old port.

As the police vehicle slowed to pick its way through barriers on the road at the destination, acrid smoke filled Mac's nostrils and irritated his eyes. A steady hiss of burning wood rose to greet him in the devastated scene. Fire trucks and official vehicles were scattered around, with curious spectators held back by uniformed soldiers and television cameras still recording everything. Sirens, sparking wood, and shouts from police and crowd merged in a confusion of sound.

Sergeant Borlak stood at the epicenter, welcomed Mac, and pointed to an old warehouse still smoldering and spitting.

"Someone torched this. We're afraid it's going to collapse even though the fire has been controlled. We can get a better look from the building across from it," Borlak said as she moved with Mac into an intact warehouse on the other side of the street from the ruin.

"And why does this involve me?" Mac asked.

"This is where NoFear was made." Borlak walked him to the roof where they could look down at the burnt shell of the laboratory. "The fire started in the early hours of the morning. Firefighters called me because it seemed to be arson. We found sophisticated drug manufacturing machines smashed and burned."

"I think I know how that happened," Mac said. "I just witnessed the autopsy on a woman named Sophie Grainger. She was involved in the manufacture of NoFear and was in the Zonguldak hospital when she died after a serious boat accident. She told me last week she wanted to stop production of NoFear."

"You think she wrecked the equipment?" Borlak asked, "then burned down the building and tried to escape by boat?"

"Maybe. I don't think there's any way of knowing," Mac said.

"What killed her?"

"That's a problem. The autopsy did not show a cause of death."

"Could it be the same kind of cardiac problem that killed Hassan?" Borlak asked.

"Certainly possible," Mac said, not mentioning the blood he had saved from the autopsy. "In a way, she was a hero. She created what she thought was a monster, but then she did what she felt was necessary to destroy it."

"Maybe she did a great service to our country by destroying this drug manufacturing plant, but maybe not. I need more information."

"Do you know who owns the laboratory?"

"Natural Supplements, Inc, but it's a shell corporation. It will take us a couple of weeks to find the real owner. I'll be sure to let you know when we have an answer."

"Does this mean I can go back to Boston?"

"Yes. That's why I called you. I accept the idea now that under the influence of NoFear, Hassan swam himself into a cardiac arrest and died. We've found no other explanation. I'll tell Hassan's mother the drug supply has been destroyed. Thank you for staying around to see this. You'll be a big hero to the family."

"I hope the supply really has been wiped out," Mac said with a frown.

"I can guarantee you it has for Istanbul. We're very good at stopping drugs."

As soon as he arrived back at his hotel, Mac arranged to travel back to Boston. Turkish Airlines had a direct flight the next day, and he snapped up the last seat on the plane.

He called home to report the plan. His thirteen-year-old daughter Maggie answered the phone. "Hi Daddy. Are you *ever* coming home? It's been days since I saw you. I did my show-and-tell about the mosques and the cats and the cisterns and the Bosporus and everything we saw in Turkey with you." She inhaled a moment and continued "And Peter got in trouble at school yesterday and Mom said it was high time you were home to discipline him and she sounds very irritated some of the time and when will you be back?"

"That's exactly why I'm calling," Mac said, trying to keep the smile from showing in his voice. "I'm arriving tomorrow. I should be there by the time you finish dinner. Is your mother there?"

He could hear Maggie shout "Mom, it's Dad. He's coming back tomorrow," and then heard Lauren's voice, restrained but vibrant. "Is that true? I'm so glad. Sometimes the children get a little rambunctious when you're not around. Will you need a ride from Logan?"

"No, I'll get a cab."

"I can't wait to see you."

Mac packed quickly, paying particular attention to the vial of blood he had taken from Sophie Grainger's autopsy. He wrapped it carefully in bubble paper and a pair of socks before shoving it into a shoe for protection. Even though it should be safe, there was always the chance he would be selected for a random search. He shuddered to think of the results, though he expected Jim Brogan would help if necessary.

The following morning, after a breakfast of pastries and strong Turkish coffee, he left for the airport.

不怕

PART TWO

NOFEAR ATTACKS AMERICA

不怕

CHAPTER THIRTEEN

MAC RETURNS TO BOSTON

BROOKLINE, MA, AND HARBOR HOSPITAL

Mac's flight landed at seven p.m. He passed through immigration easily because he had Global Entry, but he and his suitcase did not leave the customs hall until eight. His anxiety level rose as other passengers, one by one, reclaimed their bags. His was almost the last. When he pulled it off the carousel, he resisted the urge to open the suitcase in the baggage hall and see whether it had been searched.

As he exited from the customs hall, he was surprised to see his children racing toward him with ear-to-ear smiles. "Surprise!" Maggie called just before she embraced him. "You weren't expecting us to come to the airport along with Mom, were you, huh? Huh?"

"You were really late coming through," Peter added as he joined his sister in an all-encircling bear hug. "Even the pilot and flight attendants came out before you. Mom said maybe you lost your bag."

Mac looked beyond them to Lauren, standing behind the railing. Trim in jeans and cotton sweater, she waved with her own special smile. Mac felt immense gratitude. How lucky was he to have this woman as his life partner, to have this family! Bringing the children along was an unexpected bonus to her willingness to meet him at the airport.

"They wouldn't stay home," she explained, reading his mind as they headed for the Central Parking facility. "They wanted to hear about your adventures after we left Istanbul, and tell you about school, and welcome you home and—well, you'll hear for yourself."

Maggie and Peter talked non-stop during the ride, describing their school activities and other adventures since returning. Lauren drove. Mac listened and laughed.

When they arrived home, Lauren gave him a proper kiss. "And look at you," she said, putting him at arm's length. "No broken leg like Morocco, no COVID-19 like Wuhan. Just a husband returning home from an overseas conference. The kids are still crowing about exploring Istanbul the days you were at the meeting, and we just roamed around the city. I'm only sorry we couldn't fly back together."

"I already planned to be a couple of days late but got involved in another problem."

"Why am I not surprised? Does it involve Jim Brogan?"

"It does. But I asked *him* to help, not vice versa."

Lauren raised one eyebrow; a trick Mac wished he could master. "No matter," she said. 'We're ecstatic to see you. Let's just hope you're home for a while."

They ate take-out Indian food for dinner. The aroma of cardamom, spiciness of lamb vindaloo, and tang of garlic naan were old friends to Mac. They and the chatter of his children convinced him more than the plane ride that he was home.

During the meal, Mac asked each child what they liked most about their trip to Türkiye.

"Definitely the boats on the Bosporus," Peter said.

"Freighters and ferries and small motorboats. It was like a painting."

"I liked the churches, even though some of them were mosques," Maggie said. "The neatest was Hagia Sofia. It was massively impressive. Its ceilings were so high and so old— built almost two thousand years ago. It was also weird to see the Islamic shields hanging where the cross used to be."

"And what did *you* like most?" Mac asked Lauren.

"So many things. The Blue Mosque with its serenity despite the crowds, the Cisterns with the submerged Medusa, the bazaars, the Bosporus and its international sea traffic, the cats protected everywhere, the whole merging of east and west. I could go on and on. Istanbul is a spectacular city."

"I feel the same way," Mac said, pleased to have introduced his family to one of his favorite places in the world, "but nothing can beat this house right now."

Early the next morning, Mac called Dr. Grace Wu, the professor of neuropathology and neuroscience at Harbor Hospital who had directed Sophie Grainger's post-doc work. Wu did both research and clinical service in the hospital, and Mac considered her a good friend.

"Grace," he said, "I just got back from Istanbul. Met your student Sophie Grainger, but I'm sorry to tell you she died under suspicious circumstances."

"That's terrible news. What happened?"

"She had a cardiac arrest in a hospital there after seeming to be fine. I brought back a vial of her blood for biochemical analysis including a drug screen. Can I bring it to the lab later this morning?"

"Of course. I'll run it right after you get it to me."

Mac delivered the blood to Grace as soon as he arrived at the hospital.

"Sophie was so enthusiastic and smart," Grace said. "What was going on with her before she died?"

"She developed a compound called NoFear and became disenchanted with its addictive properties and tendency to lead to dangerous behaviors. We think she destroyed the Istanbul manufacturing plant and tried to escape by boat up the Bosporus, but her vessel broke up in a storm. She called me from a hospital in a remote Turkish town on the Black Sea. I got to her as fast as I could but found her dead."

"Certainly sounds suspicious," Grace said. "And the autopsy showed nothing?"

"Correct," Mac said. "There was no evidence of a fatal cardiac or brain event. I'm worried there was some drug or other metabolic cause. I hope the blood I gave you will solve the mystery of her death." He checked his watch. "My apologies for running out. I must meet with our Chief Medical Officer."

"Good luck with that," Grace said. Mac caught the sympathetic tone of her voice as he raced out the door to make it on time.

不怕

CHAPTER FOURTEEN

MAC VISITS THE CHIEF MEDICAL OFFICER

EXECUTIVE SUITE, HARBOR HOSPITAL

Mac entered the executive suite at nine a.m. for his appointment with Chief Medical Officer Brian Cook. The suite occupied the top floor of Harbor Hospital.

"He's running late," the woman at the reception desk said without apology.

"I'll come back," Mac said.

"No. Sit over there." She pointed to a chair. "I'll let you know when he can see you."

Mac sat, considering the gap that separates administrators from doctors. Administrators worry about personnel management and a complex medical reimbursement system. Did they appreciate the emotional investment doctors, nurses, and others who provide day-to-day patient care bring to their jobs? Had anyone in this office suite ever dealt with a tragedy like a malignant brain tumor in a mother of four?

For Mac, the hospital was a sacred place where tragedy and triumph battled furiously every day. Administrators, including chief medical officers, were unavoidable but sometimes did not seem to understand the stakes in caring for patients.

Cook called Mac into the office half an hour late. The room was spacious, with mementos rather than books filling the oak bookshelves. The desk placement framed Cook against a spectacular view of Boston Harbor. Several pots of artificial plants sat on tables and shelves.

"Welcome back to work, MacGregor," Cook began, waving at a chair for Mac to use. "Mind if I ask you why you extended your stay in Istanbul?"

"There was a situation I had to take care of."

"Your productivity quota suffered."

"And what exactly is my productivity quota?"

"Your PQ? You probably missed the staff meeting where I discussed it," Cook said. "It's an index of your work output. I should let you know your score is lower than most surgeons on our staff because of your travels."

"Are you suggesting there's a problem with the way I take care of patients?"

"No, no, not overall, at least when you're in town. You'll have to pay more attention to your overall PQ, though. It's an important metric for your contribution to the hospital."

He leaned toward Mac from his position across the desk as if he had something important and confidential to say. "You should especially improve your PQ if you want me to support you for the position of neurosurgeon-in-chief when neurosurgery becomes a hospital department. Max Eli, the head of the search committee for the new chief, has gathered several competitive candidates, and a lackadaisical work record could hurt you."

"I've never been called lackadaisical," Mac said. His hands clenched and unclenched at this not-so subtle attack on his patient care record. Among his many jobs as an academic surgeon, taking care of sick patients was his top priority, and he thought he was very good at it. He worked incredibly hard to make sure his patients got the best care possible.

"You don't have to worry," Cook continued with a sly smile. "I've arranged for you to cover the emergency room at Lincoln Hospital this weekend to get your numbers back on track."

Mac jumped to his feet and strode to Cook's desk. "What are you talking about? Me cover the emergency room at a suburban hospital? That's a terrible idea. I'm a neurosurgeon, not an emergency room doctor."

"Many of our other surgeons have done this," Cook said. "It's good for our relationship with the community. We want the Lincoln Hospital staff to meet our doctors as part of the outreach program. Maybe you'll even find a case you can transfer to Harbor for neurosurgery."

"It would be terrible to see an emergency neurosurgical case there," Mac said with a frown. "The hospital is not equipped for brain operations."

"Perhaps I'm not making myself clear," Cook said. "Neurosurgery is still a division of general surgery. That means your administrative boss is the chief of surgery, who has already signed off on the plan."

"You mean I have to do what he says?"

"At the moment, yes, but there is a bigger issue. When neurosurgery becomes its own independent department, I'm sure you'd like to be the chief. That position requires a team player."

"I've always worked well with other department heads," Mac said.

"Then consider covering Lincoln Hospital emergency room a demonstration of how much you'll do for the team. If you want hospital support as a candidate for the neurosurgeon-in-chief position in the new department, you'll cover the Lincoln Hospital emergency room this weekend."

Cook raised his hands as a sign of his frustration. "What's the problem anyway? Does this cut into your golf weekend?"

"I don't play golf, and this has nothing to do with my own comfort," MacGregor said, trying to contain his annoyance. He clasped and unclasped his hands again. Not long ago, he had prevented a North Korean terrorist from exploding a nuclear warhead in the hospital. Now he was just another employee taking orders from a person who appeared as blind to patient care as earlier chief medical officers.

"What if I refuse?" Mac asked.

"I'll think of something," Cook replied. "Maybe reprimand you officially for non-compliance, or if I'm really annoyed, label you as a disruptive physician." He indicated the door with a nod of his head. "Say hello to the hospital staff in Lincoln for me."

Mac spent the rest of the morning catching up with paperwork in his office. A call from Grace Wu at eleven thirty rescued him. "Mac, you've got to come down and look at this."

"On my way," he said, and arrived at her lab in five minutes.

"Sophie Grainger died of a massive heroin overdose," Wu said before he sat down.

"That can't be. She was in the hospital and had a lucid conversation with me three hours before her death. No way she could get her hands on heroin in that time. And I had no sense that she was a heroin addict."

"The mass spec doesn't lie," Wu said, "but this amount suggests a huge intravenous injection all at once. No way she would have been lucid with this concentration in her blood stream. Her blood also contains a compound I've never seen.

I'm trying to sort out what it is, but I don't think it caused her death. A whopping dose of heroin did that."

"And you're sure it was heroin that killed her?"

"Absolutely. Look at the level." She showed a chart with a huge peak even Mac could appreciate. "It is more than ten times the maximum a human can stand without respiratory arrest. At this level, the victim just stops breathing."

"Could she have injected herself with that much by mistake?"

"No. I think someone bolused it into the IV knowing it would stop her breathing. With this amount, it would only take a few minutes to die."

"But who would want her dead?" Mac mused.

"I'll leave that question to you," Wu said.

不怕

CHAPTER FIFTEEN

MAC STAFFS THE LINCOLN HOSPITAL EMERGENCY ROOM

LINCOLN HOSPITAL, LINCOLN, MA

At seven p.m. Friday, Mac reported to the emergency ward at Lincoln Community Hospital.

The blunt comments of Keisha Morris, nursing supervisor of the emergency room, mirrored his own opinions. Keisha was a mid-thirties African American woman whose authoritative air compensated for her diminutive stature. "We've put up with orthopods and cardiologists in the last few months, but you're the first neurosurgeon we've had to deal with," she said. "The program of planting you downtown specialists in our emergency room is a crock of stool."

"You may be interested to know that I agree," Mac said.

"It doesn't interest me at all."

"Understood. Can you show me the protocols for the major problems we'll have to deal with?"

She pushed a binder and a textbook toward him. "Here are guidelines for the usual emergencies we see. Migraine headaches, bicycle accidents, twisted ankles... This is a wealthy community with a lot of spoiled teenagers who go into Boston for everything including their medical care. We don't get the big trauma you downtown people have. The major challenge is to keep entitled patients from writing complaint letters to the hospital. I can help with the names of local physicians for follow-up. That doesn't mean I like the situation."

"Am I the only ER physician here?"

"Yes. A few months ago, the hospital had one of our regulars covering along with you outsiders, but apparently there wasn't enough to keep two people busy, so you're alone now. You, me, and three nurse assistants."

For the next three hours, Mac saw patients with minor problems—lacerations, allergic reactions, abdominal pain. With Keisha's help, he could manage them without much trouble. In the breaks between patients, he reviewed the protocols for managing common problems that brought people to community emergency rooms.

At midnight the Lincoln Police called to report the imminent transport of an unresponsive automobile accident victim. EMT's arrived five minutes later, doing cardiac compressions on a middle-aged Asian man strapped to a spine board.

"His whole head flops if it's left unsupported," the female EMT said.

"Was he wearing a seat belt when you found him?" Mac asked.

"No. He was pinned against the steering wheel not breathing and not moving," she replied. "His car smashed into a wall. He had no breathing or pulse and no response to our chest compressions. We weren't willing to try intubation because we think his neck is broken."

Mac did a fast examination wearing gloves, mask, and eye protection. Widely dilated pupils with no response to light. No movements of the eyes or any other part of his body to stimuli. No breathing. Mac gently manipulated the back of the neck, confirming the EMT's observation. The head flopped as if it were on a rag doll.

He at once pictured the sequence of events—unrestrained head and body bounced back and forth between steering wheel and seat back with such force the upper spine fractured and dislocated. The spinal cord was ripped or sliced, with immediate respiratory arrest followed by heart stoppage.

There was no hope of survival. "Keisha, how long before an X-ray tech can get into the hospital to confirm his broken neck? We'll need it for confirmation."

"Half an hour."

"Can you make it happen? And do you have a cervical collar?"

"Only soft," she said.

"We'll need it to maintain spine injury protocol." Mac realized stabilizing the neck made no ultimate difference in a man whose brain was dead. He still wanted to follow proper measures until the X-rays were done.

The hot line rang again. After listening for a moment, Keisha put the phone on speaker.

"Lincoln Police again. Big trouble. A teen party gone bad at one of the big houses in town. Several casualties."

"Drugs?" Mac asked, finishing the collar placement on the Asian victim. He decided to leave him at the side of the hallway in case they needed the rooms for other patients.

"Probably. We saw a bowl of pills and weed in the living room."

"Can we get extra help down here?" Mac asked Keisha.

She already had the hospital nursing supervisor on the

line. "They can spare two nurses from the inpatient wards," she said. "We can call in more if necessary once we see what's going on. There's one doctor covering the rest of the hospital. They've called in his backup."

A stretcher barreled through the door carrying a thin teenage girl. "This is Janine," the EMT said. "Still not responding despite nasal spray of Narcan. Couldn't find a vein for an IV."

The girl had gasping breaths.

Mac inserted a laryngoscope. Vomit blocked her throat. "Suction tubing," he barked.

Keisha hooked up wide bore tubing and handed it to him. Mac sucked out clotted puke, then slipped an endotracheal tube into place. The girl started to cough and reached up to grab the tube.

"She probably won't need the tube for long, but we'll need to protect her airway in case she vomits again,' Mac said to the two nurses now arriving from the wards. "Just hook her up to oxygen. And thanks for coming down to help us."

He felt his adrenalin pump as the action increased. Several ward attendants appeared, and the baseline noise escalated. "Keisha, will you stay with me and assign duties once we've seen a patient together?" Mac asked.

The arrival of another boy interrupted him. As Mac watched, the teen began rhythmic twitching of all his limbs, then became rigid and held his breath. Urine stained his pants, and he became unresponsive and flaccid. Breathing resumed normally after a few seconds, but he began to twitch again.

The crash cart appeared beside Mac. "He's still seizing. We'll need a central line," Mac said and put on sterile gloves while Keisha prepared the boy's right neck with betadine. He inserted a large-bore IV needle following the landmarks to reach the internal jugular vein. Dark venous blood spilled out before he threaded the tubing through it and connected it to a bag of sterile saline. "Ativan," he said, and injected one cc. The seizure stopped. "Put him in cubicle two and watch him for any respiratory slowing," he said to the nurses. "He may need to be intubated."

"How many more kids are there?" he asked as the EMT's headed for the door.

"At least two more. And the next ambulance is here."

The patient wheeled in on the next stretcher made Mac pause. He intuitively recognized something different about her.

"What's the story?" he asked.

"Name's Lucy Martin. Found her beside the stairs. Kids say she jumped about eight feet from a stair landing." The EMT tech pointed at a laceration in the patient's left temple. "Must have hit her head on the way down. She was awake and talking when we started, but she's not talking now."

Lucy opened her eyes after Mac called her name for the third time. He noted that her left pupil was slightly bigger than the right. When he shone a light into her left eye, the pupil constricted less briskly than the right.

"Lucy, how do you feel?"

No answer.

He shook her gently. "Lucy, wake up." She opened her eyes only slightly.

"How do you feel?"

"Headache," she mumbled.

"Can you lift both your arms for me?"

She did nothing.

He lifted her arms into the air and asked her to hold them there. The left arm stayed up, the right drifted downward

Not the pattern of a drug overdose or a seizure. Rather, the pattern of a blood clot pressing against the left side of the brain.

Neurosurgical mode engaged. This could be a life-threatening neurosurgical emergency.

Mac turned to the female EMT. "Any more details?"

She shook her head. "Maybe the kid coming in now knows. It's his house."

A stretcher burst through with two techs trying to restrain a writhing teenager. "Leave me alone," the boy shouted. "My dad will have you all fired. Get your hands off me."

"I need to know what happened to your friend Lucy," Mac said as the stretcher stopped.

"Who are you?" The boy's pupils were wide and sweat dotted his brow. "Make these assholes let go of me."

"She's very sick."

Keisha shouted that the X-Ray tech had just arrived.

The teenager looked over at Lucy. "Why is she so sleepy?"

"What happened?" Mac asked.

"Nothing. Nothing."

"Doesn't look like "nothing" to me," Mac said, pointing to Lucy lying motionless with her eyes closed.

"She decided she could fly after taking some new shit called NoFear. I couldn't stop her. Jumped off the stair landing, hit her head against a bookcase corner when she fell. Scared me because the crack sounded so loud, but then she seemed OK."

Mac knew about patients who talk and die after skull fracture. The fracture tears a hole in a blood vessel just under the skull. The vessel pumps blood into the space between the lining of the brain and the skull. At first everything seems fine. In an hour or two, the expanding clot sends the patient into a coma and kills them.

Mac began to think about the possibility of surgery.

"Do you know where her parents are?" he asked the boy.

"Hell no. Her mom's never around. Dad dropped her off at the party hours ago. Haven't seen him since."

"What other drugs were in the room?" Mac asked.

"The usual shit."

"What do you mean exactly?" Mac asked.

"Poppers, special K, X. A Chinese guy sold them to us. But the new stuff was called NoFear. We picked whatever we wanted from the bowl, but everybody got some of the new drug free. Lucy had the most."

The X-ray tech rolled the Asian man's stretcher past the boy on the way to the X-ray room. "Wait," the boy said. "That's Jimmy Wong. He's the guy who sold us all the drugs."

Mac stared after Jimmy, vowing to follow up the clear connection with NoFear. For the moment, however, he realized Lucy was moving less. He pinched her and watched her left arm respond vigorously but her right very little. He opened Lucy's eyelids. The left pupil was now larger than the right and barely constricted to bright light.

These signs meant a clot was pressing more against Lucy's brain. At Harbor Hospital he would ask for an emergency CT scan and order the operating room to prepare for a craniotomy. The scan would localize the clot precisely and he would have it out within an hour.

But this was Lincoln Hospital. "Can the X-ray tech who's here do a CT scan?" he asked Keisha.

"No. That's a different person. Why?"

Mac didn't answer. He was considering his options. *One*, send Lucy into Harbor Hospital. That would follow established protocol, but the clot would expand to flatten her brain during the transport. She would be brain dead by the time her body arrived.

Two, Mac could wait for a CT and then do surgery at this hospital, not used to emergencies. That sequence might take four hours and again leave his patient brain dead.

Three. As the final choice, Mac could violate the existing protocols of Lincoln Hospital and do surgery right now based on the physical examination. The danger with this approach was that the examination was sometimes misleading, and the surgeon could operate on the wrong side of the brain. Doing brain surgery at this hospital would also get him into political trouble.

He made his decision in two seconds.

不怕

CHAPTER SIXTEEN

BRAIN SURGERY PART ONE

EMERGENCY ROOM, LINCOLN HOSPITAL

"Remind me again how long a CT scan would take?" Mac asked Keisha. He wanted to confirm his thoughts about the limited resources at Lincoln Hospital.

She paused, looking at her watch. "The CT tech lives about a half hour away. She has to get in here, then get the machine ready. I would say about an hour and a half before the scan is done. Should I call her in?"

"We don't have that much time," Mac said with a shake of his head. "How about the operating room? How long before it could be ready?"

"About forty-five minutes."

"Call the OR team in. Do you have any neurosurgical instruments in the ER?"

"A mini bur hole kit. I've never seen it used."

"That'll do. I'll get things started." As Keisha left to make her calls and get the equipment, Mac pushed Lucy from the cubicle to the trauma room, which had an operating table and surgical light.

He rolled Lucy onto the table left side up with her head on a small pillow and pulled her luxuriant red hair over toward the right side of her head, gathering it with an elastic hair band. He used clippers to shorten the hair in front of and above her left ear. This revealed a purple bruise in the temple, which supported his suspicion of direct trauma to that region. Her long hair would cover any incision he made.

Keisha returned, looking at him with an expression that to Mac showed fear, anticipation, and excitement. The sarcastic tone had left her voice. "I notified the OR call team and the nursing supervisor. I also asked the doctor covering the hospital wards to take over the emergency room. I hope you don't mind."

"No, that's perfect. Thank you." There was no banter now in his tone or hers.

"How can I help?" she asked.

"Have you ever assisted in surgery?"

"Lacerations, small stuff."

"Do you know how to set up suction and a cautery unit?"

"Of course."

"You're an official neurosurgical nurse now. Get scrubbed." He gestured toward the sink. "Then paint antiseptic on the area I've shaved and make it into a surgical field."

He put on a hat and mask and washed his hands with antiseptic solution at the scrub sink in the trauma room. Returning to the operating table to be gowned, he found Keisha at a perfectly draped operating site, with suction, cautery, and the instruments he would need.

He marked an incision in front of the left ear, drew Xylocaine from a sterile ampule Keisha held for him, and injected it along the line he had drawn. Lucy didn't move during the injection.

"We don't have much time," he said. "This Xylocaine injection should be painful. The fact that Lucy isn't moving means brain stem compression has reached a critical point."

"Number ten scalpel please." Mac held out his hand and Keisha slapped the scalpel against it without a word. The room was silent except for the buzzing of the OR light and swooshing of the suction. He and Keshia worked in a circle of bright light surrounded by semi-darkness. The smell of prep solution reassured him, bringing him into the familiar zone of surgery. His only anxiety was for Lucy's recovery. Was this too little too late?

He incised the scalp with a deep sure cut. The edges began to bleed but with a retractor he spread the skin and sealed the pumping vessels with pressure against them. Using the cautery, he burned through the fascia and muscle and scraped the tissue away from the skull. A small fracture line was now clear in the thin temporal bone, supporting his diagnosis of a localized blood vessel tear under the fracture.

"Perforator please." Keisha again slapped the instrument into his outstretched palm. He twisted the brace and bit, producing curls of bone as he drilled the skull.

A geyser of brown fluid spurted into the air when the perforator broke through the bone.

"Epidural serum under a lot of pressure," Mac muttered. "Releasing it should buy us some time. Now the suction please." With a large bore sucker tip, he began to pull out pieces of thick clot that looked like liver slices.

A strident voice interrupted him, booming over the hissing suction.

"What are you doing?"

Mac turned to see a tall woman with "Supervisor" embroidered on her white coat. She stood with fists on her hips and legs spread in a defiant pose.

"Ms. Nordstrom, our evening nursing supervisor," Keisha said without looking up.

"Please put on a hat and mask and stay where you are," Mac said, continuing to focus on the operative field.

"Who are you? Is that brain surgery? Here in my emergency room?" Nordstrom asked.

"Please put on your mask and hat," Mac repeated.

Nordstrom slapped on a head covering and held a mask in front of her as she headed toward the operating table. She stopped as she saw the fragments of clot piled on the instrument table.

"This is against hospital policy. We send our neurosurgical patients into Harbor Hospital."

"This girl would never make it that far."

"That's your opinion. Where's your evidence?"

Mac held up his suction with a large chunk of congealed blood hanging from it. "This is all the evidence we need," he said. "Epidural clot. And I must give you even worse news. We're going to do a craniotomy in the operating room upstairs in a couple of minutes to take out the rest of the clot and make sure the bleeding doesn't start again. This is just a stopgap."

"That's impossible. We don't do brain surgery here. You're Dr. MacGregor, right? From Harbor Hospital? Are you even on staff?" the supervisor said.

"I had to get full staff privileges to cover the emergency room. Check with your chief of surgery. Tonight, your hospital is going to do brain surgery for the first time. Just get out of my surgical field so you don't infect the patient. Please."

Mac valued his reputation for calm handling of any operative complication, but officious meddling with what needed to be done for a patient made him furious. Even at Harbor Hospital, he spent his most frustrating hours advocating for patient-oriented care.

"You can't talk to me like that. I'm the supervisor here."

"And you just might help save this teenager's life. Keisha, do you have a status for the OR?"

"They just texted. They're ready. The anesthesiologist is upstairs waiting, and nurses are opening a surgical kit."

Movement under the surgical drapes interrupted the interchange. Lucy's right arm appeared, stretched out beyond the drapes. "We need to get to the OR quickly now. We can't seal the bleeding artery with this small opening. It will keep pumping," Mac said.

He left the retractors in place as he packed the incision with antiseptic sponges, then covered the area with sterile bandages and a white turban. "She's waking up since we took out part of the clot, which is wonderful news. We need to get her intubated and finish the job to keep the responsible artery from bleeding again. Keisha, disconnect the suction and cautery. We're moving up to the OR."

He looked back at the supervisor as they passed her, standing with open mouth and furious eyes. Lucy now thrashed on the bed, twisting her head as Mac tried to restrain her. "Go ahead and call the surgeon-in-chief or any other official you want," Mac said. "Lucy has only one chance to live, and we're going to give it to her now."

不怕

CHAPTER SEVENTEEN

BRAIN SURGERY PART TWO

OPERATING ROOM, LINCOLN HOSPITAL, LINCOLN, MA

Mac and Keisha wheeled Lucy into the operating room, where brilliant illumination turned darkness into day. The clinking of instruments, hissing of the suction tubing, buzzing of OR lights, and murmuring voices welcomed Mac to an environment he knew well. The smell of antiseptic hovered in the room. The floor glistened in the corners from recent mopping.

A male scrub nurse, gowned and masked, stood by an open instrument tray preparing towels and drapes for surgery. A circulating nurse scurried about connecting cords and suction tubing. A woman in scrubs but not gowned twirled dials on the anesthesia machine and arranged an endotracheal tube and laryngoscope on its surface.

They turned toward him in unison as he entered.

"Dr. MacGregor?" the woman said. "I'm Dr. Tina Sundaram, the anesthesiologist on call." She nodded toward the others. "John, our scrub nurse, Nancy, our circulator."

"Yes, I'm MacGregor," Mac said. "Thanks for coming in so fast. This is Lucy Martin, a teenager with a left temporal epidural hematoma. I removed part of the clot in the emergency room. She needs a craniotomy to remove the rest and seal the bleeding artery."

"Can we do this surgery here? Shouldn't we send her to Harbor?" Sundaram asked. She looked over at the patient, head covered in a swath of gauze, still twisting on the bed. Blood seeped through the dressing and dripped onto the sheets. "What's under the dressing?" Sundaram asked with a frown.

"Blood clot, a skull opening, and a bleeding artery," Mac said. "No way she'd survive the ambulance ride." Mac began tapping his right foot. Could these people not understand the urgency of the situation?

"Do we have surgical consent? Has anyone reached the family?" Sundaram asked.

"The ER is locating them."

Sundaram put down the endotracheal tube. "I can't anesthetize her if we don't have consent. It's against hospital bylaws. Could be considered assault and battery."

Mac knew Sundaram was right. He also knew the solution, hammered out for just this situation.

"The administrator on call can give proxy consent," Mac said. "Dr. Sundaram, you intubate Lucy while I get temporary approval. You're covered in any case. The intubation is necessary to protect her airway even if we don't do surgery."

Sundaram turned back toward the patient as the circulating nurse called the administrator of the day. Mac moved to hold Lucy's hands for the intubation.

A strong female voice boomed through the speakerphone two minutes later.

"Linda Ward, administrator on call. Who is this?"

"Dr. Duncan MacGregor."

"Do I know you, Dr. MacGregor?"

"No; I'm covering the emergency room as part of the neighborhood outreach of Harbor Hospital."

"How can I help?"

"We have a seventeen-year-old girl with an epidural hematoma. We haven't been able to find her parents and must remove the clot right now."

"Brain surgery? We don't do brain surgery at Lincoln Hospital. Not in our accreditation."

"If this girl dies because you forbid surgery, more than your accreditation will be at risk. I expect you'll have a lot of lawyers to talk to as well as reporters from the Boston Globe. And your boss."

"You don't have to be so offensive."

"A teenager's life is at stake. I just want to remove the clot. Will you give me permission to go ahead?"

"Yes. Don't screw up."

"Thank you." Mac turned away from the phone and returned to the operating table. His heart was pounding both from the imminent surgery and from the fact that an administrative denial might have caused this girl's death.

He removed the turban, sterile dressing, and antiseptic packing to reveal the small hole he had made, with the retractors still in place holding back the scalp edges.

Thick clot had already refilled the space under the bone.

"If you wonder why we're operating up here when we just took out clot in the ER, this is the reason," he said to the OR team. "The artery causing the clot is still pumping and has almost refilled the cavity. We have to seal it off directly."

He lengthened the incision and stopped any bleeding skin vessels with electrocautery. The acrid smell of singed tissue filled the operative field. The inhalation and exhalation of the ventilator and the suction's loud hissing created a background for his minimalist requests.

"Perforator," he muttered.

The scrub nurse handed him the brace and bit and he made two new bone holes with it.

"Gigli saw." He slid what looked like a long wire under the bone between adjacent holes and pulled it back and forth until it sawed through the bone. After three cuts, he lifted the bone.

Now he could see the entire red clot compressing the lining of the brain. The portion he had scooped out in the emergency room remained visible as a fraction of the whole. Sliding a curved dissector along the dura, he gradually lifted the firm mass from the glistening white membrane that still protected the brain.

"All outside the dura, as we hoped," he said, lifting a mass the consistency of cranberry jelly and depositing it on the specimen tray.

Where it had lifted from the dura, a blood vessel spurted blood into the air.

"Middle meningeal artery," Mac said. "This is the cause of the bleeding." He held the bone he had removed over the opening to show how the fracture lay exactly over the tear in the blood vessel. "Torn by the fracture. No way that would have stopped on its own. Bipolar cautery please."

He pressed the blades of the forceps-shaped instrument together and the bleeding stopped with a buzz.

"We're done," Mac said after he washed the field, sutured the bone in place, stitched the muscle and fascia, closed the galea, and sutured the skin. It took him fifteen minutes to close.

As he wrapped the dressing around the girl's head, the operating room staff stood silently, like parishioners at prayer. "That whole procedure took thirty minutes," the anesthesiologist said. "It'll take longer than that to wake her up."

"We've got all night now," Mac said. "No rush at all." He took a seat at the corner of the OR, knowing he should start dictating the operative note. Instead, he sat and wondered what kind of drug would make a seventeen-year-old girl jump off a stairway landing.

不怕

CHAPTER EIGHTEEN

LUCY'S FAMILY

LINCOLN HOSPITAL

After Lucy had been transported safely to the intensive care unit, Mac returned to the emergency ward exhausted.

The ER chaos had dissipated. The day shift had begun and only a few routine patients sat waiting to be seen. With everything under control, Mac wanted only to be sure his patient was all right, then go home and forget the complexities of the night he had just passed.

"I'm Duncan MacGregor," he said to the group at the nurses' station. "Do you need anything from me to sign out?"

The nurse in charge, a thirty-something man, said with a smile. "No sir. You're already a legend here."

Mac proceeded to the surgeon's lounge to shower and shave. When he returned to the ICU, he found Lucy extubated, head propped on three pillows. The usual mixture of nurses, residents, and respiratory therapists swirled around him.

Mac thanked the anesthetist for removing Lucy's endotracheal tube so efficiently and leaned over to speak quietly in his patient's ear.

"Hi Lucy," he said. "I'm Dr. MacGregor. How are you feeling?"

"Headache." she said slowly, her voice hoarse from the endotracheal tube that had just been removed. She opened her eyes. "What happened? Where am I?"

Mac took both her hands in his. "You jumped from a stair landing, fractured your skull, and got a blood clot over your brain. You have arm and leg bruises that may hurt, but nothing else is broken. We did some Xrays while you were asleep. I had to do an operation to take the clot out. You're at Lincoln Hospital. The headache'll get better. Your parents should be here soon."

"Only my dad," she said. "My mom's in D.C."

"Would you do me a favor. Could you try to hold up your arms like this?" Mac lifted both his arms to shoulder height.

Lucy tried to do the same, but the right arm sagged a few inches "You still have some weakness, but you'll be OK in a day or so," Mac said. "Just to be sure, we'll be moving you to Harbor Hospital later today."

"It can't be soon enough for me," a male voice said behind Mac. "I take my daughter to a party and the next thing I know she gets brain surgery without my consent."

Mac swiveled around. A man in his forties with tailored suit, white shirt, and red tie stood with fists on his hips glaring at him. "Are you Mr. Martin?" Mac asked. "We tried to reach you before going ahead with the emergency surgery. Lucy would not have done well if we waited any longer."

"You must not have tried hard. And don't try to tell me my daughter was taking some drug. That's not her style."

"Hi Dad," Lucy said with no emotion but opening her eyes.

"Don't worry, sweetheart," the man said as he turned toward her. "We'll get you to a real hospital soon." He turned back to Mac. "You the surgeon?"

"Yes. Duncan MacGregor." He extended his hand. "I'm—"

"Never mind who you are. We'll have the head of neurosurgery at Harbor Hospital take over from here."

"That would be me," Mac said, trying to restrain his temper. He was too tired for this kind of antagonism.

"What the hell are you doing at Lincoln Hospital? This is just a local facility, not a real hospital."

Mac shrugged. "Inter-hospital politics. And you are?"

"Obviously Lucy's father, Bruce Martin. Also, a senior partner at Kohn Leaven."

Mac winced. This firm had the most aggressive lawyers in New England for bringing malpractice cases.

"Can we step outside and discuss what happened?" Mac asked Mr. Martin, looking over at Lucy.

She had closed her eyes and seemed to be asleep.

Mac led Martin to the family area and described the events of the previous evening. "Of course, I will seek several other opinions about your actions," Mr. Martin said, "and you had better be prepared to talk with my ex-wife. She'll be here this afternoon."

"Tell her to meet us at Harbor Hospital. Lucy should be transferred by noon."

"I won't be there. I'm much too busy," he said. "I'm due in court in an hour."

Mac made the preparations for Lucy's transfer to Harbor Hospital himself. He followed the ambulance en route and decided he'd best wait in his office until Lucy's mother came. If she was anything like her husband, he was in for another terrible hour.

At three p.m. the ICU notified Mac that Lucy's mother had arrived. Mac was tired and still upset by Mr. Martin's attitude but went directly to the intensive care unit.

Two men stood at the door. Black suits and earpieces suggested Secret Service.

"Are you protecting someone?" Mac asked as he approached.

"Not your business," the man with a crew cut said. "Who are you?"

Mac showed his ID. "I'm here to see Lucy Martin. I'm her surgeon."

"We're here with her mother. I assume you know she's POTUS' Chief of Staff."

Mac shook his head as he approached Lucy's cubicle. How complicated was the fallout from this surgery going to be? The chief medical officer of the hospital had already ordered him to meet about the case the next morning, and Lucy's father might file a malpractice suit claiming lack of informed consent. Now the child's mother turned out to be one of the most powerful people in the country, the person who controlled access to the president.

Entering Lucy's cubicle, Mac saw a thirty-something red-headed woman holding Lucy's hand. Her hair was bobbed, her blue suit fitted perfectly, and she looked as if she had been crying.

"Dr. MacGregor?" she asked as Mac arrived, standing to greet him.

"Yes. You're Mrs. Martin?"

"Not anymore, but I am Lucy's mother. Janice Lake." She extended her hand. "I want to thank you for saving my daughter's life. Before I left Washington this morning my ex-husband told me what happened at Lincoln Hospital. A lot of surgeons might have tried to avoid the mess that you've probably gotten into politically, but I believe it is because of you my daughter is alive today." She smiled with apparent genuine warmth.

Mac looked at the floor. "Well, it was a complicated situation."

Janice touched his arm and said "Could we step outside for a moment? There are some questions I'd like to ask in private."

Mac led her to a family room sequestered from the rest of the ward, sitting beside the nurse's station. The Secret Service men followed but stayed outside.

"I've prepared a short letter expressing my gratitude for what you've done," she said, handing him an envelope marked with the White House imprint. Mac slipped it into his pocket with an embarrassed "thank you."

Questions followed in a barrage. "Why did Lucy decide to jump? Was her brain severely bruised? Will she have permanent brain damage? What can we expect over the next few weeks?"

Mac invited her to sit. "I don't know why she jumped, but one of the other kids said she shouted something like "Look? I'm not scared!" just before she leaped off the landing. We are doing a detailed analysis of her blood to see what drugs or other chemicals may be in it."

"Will you let me know as soon as you have any results?"

"Of course. I can say that her brain was probably not bruised. The good thing about this kind of clot is that it presses between the skull and the dura, the brain's outside layer. The brain itself does not get exposed to blood, which makes a dramatic difference."

"How long do we have to worry about something bad happening?"

"About a month. If she's OK by then, she should have no other problems. I'm sure you're thinking of seizures, but those are not common after an epidural hematoma if surgery is done in time. We'll get MRI and CT scans to follow her brain's recovery. We have a portable CT scanner in the unit. The scan taken earlier today showed no residual clot and a brain that looked good."

"I've taken a week off to be with Lucy. How long will she be in the hospital?"

"That depends. Will she stay with her father in Lincoln when she leaves?" Mac asked, trying to hide his distaste for Bruce Martin.

Janice smiled. "Bruce's not so bad, really. We're divorced, but still have an amicable relationship. In my job with the President, I couldn't give him and Lucy the attention they needed, and he couldn't tolerate that."

She stared at the wall, then seemed to force herself back to the conversation. "Anyway, what's done is done. I'll stay with Lucy at Bruce's house until you think she's ready to be on her own."

"If she's under your care, she could probably leave the hospital in three days."

"Will I see you again before she leaves?"

"Twice a day. I make rounds at seven in the morning and five-thirty in the afternoon and you can reach me on the cell phone any time." He handed her his card with his cell number scribbled on the back.

"Thank you, Dr. MacGregor," Janice said and stood, suggesting to Mac he had answered her questions.

They returned to Lucy, still sleeping naturally. Mac, thinking of his own daughter, had tears in his eyes as he left the ICU. He knew more than anyone how close Lucy had come to death.

He drove home and fell asleep on the living room couch.

His thirteen-year-old daughter Maggie woke him. "Daddy, wake up. You're famous." She flicked on the television, pumping the volume way too high.

"Boston brain surgeon saves teenager's life" proclaimed the rolling banner of the five o'clock local news. The reporters described how emergency brain surgery had been done at Lincoln Hospital for the first time by Dr. Duncan MacGregor. The patient, whose name could not be released for HIPAA reasons, was resting comfortably and appeared to be recovering uneventfully.

The commentators presented a whirl of questions about the ability of community hospitals to handle true emergencies. "What would have happened if Dr. MacGregor had not been on call?" the reporter asked.

Mac groaned as Maggie pummeled him. He rolled over, embarrassed by the publicity.

不怕

CHAPTER NINETEEN

CHIEF MEDICAL OFFICER MEETING TWO

EXECUTIVE SUITE, HARBOR HOSPITAL

"I send you to cover one emergency room for one night," Brian Cook said, glaring from Mac to a pile of papers on his desk. "And I get a stack of incident reports from the hospital."

"So quickly?" Mac asked, standing in front of Cook's desk. "I can never get an administrative action in less than a month."

Cook looked at him with narrowed eyes. "Yes, so fast. And from people important to our outreach program."

"Who exactly are these people?"

"The nursing supervisor for the emergency room, the administrator on call, the Lincoln hospital president," Cook picked up three thick packets. "And they've sent detailed documentation. The only different report was from a nurse named Keisha, who said you were unbelievably great in an impossible situation. She said she was risking her job writing the letter, but she wanted me to know how valuable a doctor you are."

"The patient would have died if I didn't operate."

"That's a matter for our review committee to address. All I know is that you hijacked an operating room and its staff to do surgery that had no place at that community hospital. The administrators there are furious, and we're not very happy here either. They may decide to hire neurosurgeons of their own, leaving us out of the loop."

Mac had anticipated this meeting when he made the decision to operate. To him, it reflected the perpetual tension between hospital administrators, who spent their time avoiding controversy, and doctors, who had to take care of real patients. A year ago, he would have stomped out of the room or exploded in anger. Now he paused to frame his answer.

Cook seemed unnerved by the silence. "Well, what do you have to say for yourself?"

Mac slipped the envelope Janice had given him from his pocket and passed it to Cook.

"The patient's mother thought hospital administration might criticize what I did. I guess she's pretty used to political messes. Here's her comment."

Cook stared at the White House monogram on the envelope and sliced it open with an opener from his desk. He read it for a few seconds and looked up at Mac.

"Jesus, MacGregor. This is huge. I had no idea who this kid was. What a coup for Harbor to have had you there when you were needed! The President's chief of staff seems to think you walk on water. I'm going to send this letter to our Board of Trustees."

"Make a copy of it. I'm going to keep the original, since it's addressed to me," Mac said, putting his hand out to get the letter back. "I am sorry you got the complaints. All I know is the emergency surgery was necessary. Harbor Hospital got positive publicity. Everyone still acknowledges it's one of the best places in the United States to have a neurosurgical operation." *And it's your job to deal with the complaints. My job is to try to save lives.*

不怕

CHAPTER TWENTY

THE SECRET OF NOFEAR

NEUROPATHOLOGY OFFICE, HARBOR HOSPITAL

Mac let Lucy go home under her mother's care four days after the surgery. He asked for a Zoom call every evening until they met face-to-face again ten days postoperatively. Both Janice Lake and Bruce Martin were at that meeting. Mac removed the sutures, and on detailed neurological examination found only slightly less good fine finger movement in the right hand than in the left. There were no other issues.

"You're doing great," Mac said to Lucy. "You can go back to school, shampoo, and let your hair cover the incision. Just don't hit your head any time soon."

"Having an obvious incision was the only thing I worried about when I started to recover," Lucy said with a grin. "And I'm not much of a sports person, so don't worry about me hitting my head. I'll be extra careful."

The family discussed what activities Lucy could safely join in and left chatting amiably. Mac was pleased and surprised at Bruce Martin's farewell, "You did a good job, MacGregor. Thank you."

A week later, Dr. Grace Wu asked Mac to meet her in the Neuropathology section of the hospital to examine the brain of Jimmy Wong, the drug dealer for the partygoers in Lincoln who had died in a car crash.

With a noticeable increase in his heart rate, Mac surveyed the autopsy suite as he entered. An operating room energized him. An autopsy room left him anxious. Here doctors met their failures.

Six gleaming stainless-steel tables dotted the space, with a sloping tile floor and drains for blood and other bodily fluids. Cubicles for frozen corpses lined the walls. Harsh fluorescent lighting and the smell of disinfectant created an unpleasant mixture of strong olfactory sensations.

He stared down at the two corpses Wu had put out in front of him. "I assume you have the story on Wong and how he got here," Wu said.

"He apparently supplied drugs to the kid throwing the party," Mac said. "When things got out of hand and the police arrived, he jumped in his car to escape. Sped along Bedford Road and at the junction with Route 2 overturned the car. We thought he fractured his C1-2 vertebrae and died instantly. Never buckled his seat belt."

"That's even more detailed than the story I had. I want you to see the changes in his brain," Wu said, wearing a mask, hat, gloves, and surgical gown. "I'm going to show you two bodies to compare."

She moved to the head of one of the tables. "Our first corpse is man with a long history of narcotic use who died of a typical heroin overdose." She ripped away the sheet to reveal a thin man with skin as pale as the sheet that had covered him. Thrombosed veins and needle marks scarred his arms, feet, and neck. She opened his mouth revealing rotting teeth. "Even his tongue had the signs of multiple injections. This is a man without hope, an end-stage drug abuser."

"Now compare him with Jimmy Wong." She pulled the sheet back to the chest of the second corpse. "Not cachectic like our other victim. No needle marks. Looks like a normal businessperson. And you're right, he died from a severe brain injury to the respiratory center after C1-2 dislocation. The important finding is what these two victims have in common. Let's go to my office." She moved to the edge of the autopsy room, removing her gown and gloves.

Mac followed without protest. As a neuroscientist, neuropathologist, and friend, Wu often used her knowledge of brain chemistry to help Mac sort out difficult problems. She had a large helping of the surgeon's mentality in her makeup, eager to find a decisive solution to whatever problem faced her.

"Do you remember the DEA classification of drugs?" Wu asked as they walked down the hallway.

"I think so. Not so sure about Schedule three and above."

"Keep in mind Schedule two drugs like fentanyl, cocaine, and oxycodone for the next half hour."

Wu's office was small but carefully organized. Books and journals stood like soldiers on the shelves, with jars filled with brain specimens dotted between them. Flowering jasmine created a scent that belied the function of the rest of the space. Like Wu herself, the office occupied a pivotal location between Pathology and Neuroscience in Harbor Hospital.

"Let me guess. You believe that NoFear has characteristics of an addictive drug?" Mac asked.

"Yes, except it's not marketed as a drug so it's not subject to FDA or DEA regulations," Wu replied. "The manufacturers claim it is merely a nutritional supplement. That means it's not regulated the same way medications are. It can be distributed to the whole population including children without interference."

"How is that possible?" Mac asked. "Surely some supplements are as dangerous as any drug."

"It's a huge hole in consumer protection opened by lobbyists who got the Dietary Supplement Health and Education Act passed in 1994. Since then, supplements have become a fifty billion dollar a year business. But let's look at how NoFear affects the brain."

Wu sat down at her computer, flipped on a projector, and doused the room lights. A holographic model labelled "synaptic membrane" rotated before them.

"Looks like purple spaghetti between two slices of Swiss cheese," Mac said.

"That's a typical surgeon's description if I ever heard one," Grace laughed. "Did you miss breakfast this morning? No, it's not cheese. It's a model of the nerve membrane where it receives input from other nerve cells. The spaghetti is a benzodiazepine receptor waiting for something to attach to it."

"And NoFear does that attachment?" Mac asked. "What do the Swiss cheese slices represent?"

"Layers of a nerve cell membrane, and the holes are channels in the membrane. Without a benzodiazepine molecule like Valium around them, the receptors hang in a twisted tangle as you see them here."

"What does benzodiazepine do when it attaches?"

"Watch. The benzodiazepine molecule is red." Grace pressed a computer key and the hologram changed. The tangle of spaghetti tightened into a ball around the red molecule as if it had been twirled on a fork. The ball now fell into a hole in the cheese and blocked it.

"Sealing these channels prevents the cell from responding to electrical signals from other cells," Wu said.

"So those specific neurons became unable to receive impulses from other neurons?"

"Exactly, and if those impulses carry a fear message, the person owning the brain has no fear. This so-called dietary supplement has the same effect as drugs like Valium and Librium, but is much stronger."

"So NoFear is in fact a psychoactive drug."

"According to this modelling, one of the strongest anxiolytics we know of." She flicked on an image of the human brain with hundreds of dots. "These are places in the brain where neurons have benzodiazepine receptors. As you can see, they are all over the brain in a widespread system of neural suppression. If they are all blocked, the result is to remove fear."

Grace smiled at Mac's open-mouthed stare. "But there's more. Let me show you a postmortem study on the heroin addict." She opened a jar on her desk and let a slice of brain about five millimeters thick and two centimeters in diameter fall onto a tray in front of Mac. "This is a brain slice taken through this man's brain stem at the level of the fourth ventricle. We did some special stains to show its state of activation."

A small area of the brain had a slight blue color.

"Our old friend the locus coeruleus," Mac said. "It's the center for noradrenalin in the brain and sends neurons almost everywhere. When it is activated, a person is anxious, ready to fight. When it is quiet, the brain and the person containing it are tranquil. Some neuroscientists think alcohol, narcotics, gambling, and sex addiction all activate this same area of the brain to produce their addictive effects."

"For a surgeon, you remember a lot of neurochemistry," Wu said. "Look at a normal brain." She flashed up a hologram with a bright blue band on the floor of the fourth ventricle. "Now look at the same area from both our victims in the morgue."

An image identical to that of the heroin addict flashed onto the screen.

"My God," Mac said, standing and beginning to pace. His heart raced as the implications of what he was seeing struck him. "It looks as if NoFear does the same thing to the brain as heroin, the most dangerous narcotic we know. Does that mean it's likely to be hugely addictive?" The memory of Sophie Grainger's description of her attempt to stop NoFear flashed into his mind.

"Yes, and it does more," Wu said. "Even if someone is not addicted, it will make them ignore the whole set of fear signals humans have developed to avoid dangerous or illegal actions."

Mac ran his fingers through his hair. "So, this so-called dietary supplement is as addictive as heroin and is extremely dangerous because of the disinhibition it causes."

"Exactly," Wu said. "The big questions are why it's being advertised as a simple herbal remedy for anxiety and who is behind its marketing?"

不怕

CHAPTER TWENTY-ONE

THE NEW CHINESE PLAN

KEMPINSKI HOTEL, ISTANBUL, TÜRKIYE

This setting is glorious, Jin thought as he surveyed the scene from the Kempinski Cafe. The Bosporus lay a few meters away, with ferries and container ships dotting its sparkling blue expanse. Throughout the café, potted magnolias and laurel added color to the white furniture and linen tablecloths of the restaurant. The Asian shore and Princess Tower beckoned across the water. Occasional sirens from sea traffic punctuated the mid-morning silence. The aroma of Turkish coffee and freshly baked pastries filled the air under the outdoor canopy.

Except for my breakfast companion.

Jin's boss Han sat across from Jin, alternately downing champagne and stuffing *kunefe* and *su boregi* into his mouth. The sweet pastries disappeared as if by magic.

Han's appearance in Istanbul signaled how important the NoFear project was to Chinese leaders but filled Jin with dread. If he made a mistake, Han and his colleagues would eliminate him with a wave of a hand.

"I want to congratulate you for dealing with the problem of Sophie Grainger," Han said. "After the destruction of the Istanbul plant and the current complexities of Turkish politics, we are going to move our NoFear production and distribution facilities to the United States. After all, that's the country we want to destabilize." He signaled to the waiter to refill his glass of Dom Perignon and bring more pastries.

"We may have difficulty getting the drug approved by the FDA in America," Jin said, apprehensive about the strict regulatory climate. He had spent considerable time researching the rules for compounds like NoFear in the USA as part of his English studies.

"That makes no difference. We will market NoFear as a dietary supplement, making the FDA powerless. It has little jurisdiction over proprietary food supplements."

"But could it change its mind? Could it declare NoFear a drug?"

"You worry too much," Han said, frowning as he sipped his third glass of morning champagne. "Sterling Underwood, our very persuasive lobbyist, will make certain NoFear remains a dietary supplement for at least our lifetimes."

Jin decided he had better change the topic. "Where is the new manufacturing facility?" he asked, hiding his annoyance that his superiors had excluded him from the selection of the new site.

Lowering his eyes, he stared at his Turkish coffee, so much better than the watery beverage called coffee in China. It was important not to appear too aggressive in asking one's superior questions.

"Somerville, a suburb of Boston north of Cambridge," Han said. "It's the up-and-coming city for biotechnology. Kendall Square in Cambridge has priced itself out of manufacturing space. Our analysts have been reviewing possible sites for weeks."

He smiled with obvious pride at the site selection he and

his peers had made. Jin thought the smile was more gloating than friendly. It increased the psychic distance between them. Han was fat and old and lazy, but he held such an important role in the Council there was no way to get around him.

Jin could only stare like a dog waiting for a bone until his boss continued. "Of course, our administrative offices will be in Cambridge with all the big players. It sits in Kendall Square right beside Novartis and Pfizer and Google and Microsoft. That gives us immediate credibility."

"And who—"

"Naturally you want to know who we have chosen to run the facility," Han said, interrupting Jin to pre-empt the question burning the tip of his tongue. "Obviously, it's not you, or I would have discussed the matter with you long before this. We have recruited a perfect New England businessperson named Thaddeus Lowell to run the office as apparent CEO. He will do nothing without my approval. You will work with him in product marketing and distribution."

Han smiled as he attacked a new basket of assorted pastries. "Our Washington lobbyist Underwood is steadily adding important people to our list of converts. Next month he hosts a party that includes a Supreme Court justice, a leading congressman, a prominent TV host, and many opinion leaders. They will all try NoFear after that party and become addicted."

"And if they don't?" Jin said almost by reflex.

Han slammed his fat fist on the table and stared across at Jin. "You doubt me? You think I don't know what I'm doing?"

Jin recoiled, suddenly fearful. "N-no sir, that is not what I was suggesting."

"You question my knowledge of America and perhaps even my wisdom in general?"

"No sir, I would never do that," Jin said, beginning to tremble.

"Listen carefully to your responsibility." Han said. "You must market and distribute NoFear throughout the United States, never letting it get back to China. Let me repeat. *It must never get back into China.*" He licked his fingers. "NoFear consumption will become an epidemic in the United States. Underwood will make sure that enough Congressmen and Justices are users to block any attempts to regulate it."

He finished the bottle of Dom Perignon, wrapped two pastries in a cloth napkin, and stuffed them into his pocket.

"May I ask one final question, please?" Jin said. "Wouldn't addicted politicians just go to rehab and recover, then be very eager to block the drug?"

He realized asking was a mistake as soon as the words left his lips.

Han waved a finger in Jin's face. "Again, you doubt me! The special people Underwood is targeting believe they know everything. They shun negative publicity and will do anything to keep their addiction secret."

He stood to leave. "Of course, we will have millions of common citizens taking NoFear as well. It is the proletariat who will begin the civil war. Make sure you take care of my breakfast bill."

不怕

CHAPTER TWENTY-TWO

NATURAL SUPPLEMENTS INC.

HARBOR HOSPITAL AND CAMBRIDGE, MA

"I've identified the American source of NoFear," Mac said to Grace Wu the day after they reviewed the devastating effect of the compound on the brain. She sat across from him on an overstuffed chair in his Harbor Hospital office, barely able to find space between journals and other papers piled on every available surface.

"Please forgive the mess," Mac continued. "My grant renewal is due in two weeks. I have to be sure I haven't missed any important references in preparing it. Can I offer you coffee? Tea?"

Seeing her shake her head, he continued. "The parent company is called Natural Supplements Inc., with its head office in Cambridge. I'd like to visit it to be sure the leadership understand what their compound does. It seems only fair to go them directly before we seek a higher authority like the FDA. They may not know their compound is addictive. Would you join me? Perhaps we can convince them to modify their product or even take it off the market."

"Of course, I'll go with you," Grace said, "but I don't think there's much chance of the company removing NoFear voluntarily. It's too popular. I just found out my executive assistant takes it every day. He said it helps his chronic anxiety. In a rather snotty comment, he added that I should try it rather than denounce it." She sat more upright in the chair, physically stiffening. "I described its potential for addiction and dangerous effects, told him he might have to leave if he felt that strongly about it."

"And?" Mac asked.

"He shouted that I couldn't dismiss him for taking a dietary supplement, especially one that everyone else uses."

"Exactly what we were worried about," Mac said. "That kind of response is typical for people taking NoFear. They don't seem to care about the consequences of their actions."

He stood and began to pace. "And there's more to worry about. Natural Supplements Inc. manufactures NoFear, but several shell organizations obscure its ownership. I couldn't trace them, so I asked my CIA friend Jim Brogan to investigate its origins."

"Which country? Russia or China?" Grace asked.

Mac stared at her and began to laugh. "China, in fact the Chinese Politburo. The company CEO is an American named Tad Lowell, but he is just a spokesperson for the Chinese communist party. I have to admit they've picked classy surroundings—corporate office in Kendall Square, with the manufacturing plant in Boynton Yards in Somerville. I've made an appointment to meet with Lowell tomorrow."

"How did you manage that?" Wu asked.

"When I first called, Lowell's executive assistant said the only available slot would be three months from now. I told him I had information about the addictive effects of NoFear. Apparently, those were magic words. A slot appeared tomorrow morning at eleven."

To get to Kendall Square the next morning, Mac and Grace took the MBTA Silver Line to South Station and Red Line to Kendall/MIT. Driving or taking an Uber would be filled with delays because of the omnipresent bike lanes that narrowed all Cambridge streets, making the morning rush hour a nightmare.

As they exited from the Kendall station, they joined throngs of young people with backpacks and earbuds. The press of the crowd, pelotons of bicyclists in front of them, and shouted conversations reminded Mac of Cambridge England, a city he had visited often to meet with professional colleagues.

Directly ahead of them, a building with the signature "Natural Supplements Inc." nestled beside Google, Apple, Microsoft, and the MIT Museum.

The all-glass front door swung open automatically as they entered a foyer with streaming videos of robust young men and women engaging in sculling, basketball, and soccer. They all touted the benefits of NoFear. At the reception desk, a enthusiastic woman with a perfect figure enhanced by a white jogging suit greeted them with a smile. She checked their driver's licenses and went with them to the elevator, wishing them a great day as they began their ascent.

The executive reception area featured six oversized beanbag chairs. An immaculately groomed young man sat at a white desk and welcomed them with a smile. "So lovely to see you on this wonderful day. Tad will be with you in a moment. May I get you sparkling water, herbal tea, or organic cranberry juice?"

"Thank you. I think we're fine," Mac said, turning to Grace. She nodded in agreement.

The door at the end of the room opened to reveal a tanned

male with a scruff beard, slightly gray temples, bespoke blue silk suit, and Gucci shoes. He greeted them with a smile that reminded Mac of a movie idol's and invited them into his office.

The space exuded light, looking over the Charles River with Boston on one side and Kendall Square on the other. A conference table, computer monitors, potted plants, and posters extolling the benefits of NoFear completed the décor. New Age music added to the serene atmosphere, and the scent of jasmine far beyond the output of the few plants present permeated the space.

"Lovely to welcome you to NoFear headquarters," the CEO said. "I'm Thaddeus Lowell—call me Tad—and I want to say at the outset I am honored to greet such distinguished guests from the premier hospital in the country. How can I help you?"

"Thank you for seeing us so quickly," Mac said. "We thought the situation was urgent because of information about NoFear we'd like to share with you."

"Of course, but first please sit and let me point out how wonderful our product is." He pointed to overstuffed chairs facing a large LED screen.

"NoFear removes anxiety and creates a state of quiet euphoria, allowing an untroubled existence," Lowell continued. "The people of America have welcomed it to alleviate the discomfort of daily life." He clicked a remote and projected a map of the United States onto a screen. "We sell one million pills a day. As you can see, New York, Los Angeles, Chicago, and Washington are the major markets."

"We have evidence that the compound may be addictive," Mac interrupted.

"What evidence?"

"It activates the locus coeruleus," Mac said.

"And why should I care about that?" Lowell said, stiffening.

"Any compound that activates that nucleus is likely to be addictive." Wu said. "It's an area of the brain associated with pleasure-seeking behavior."

"Do you have hard evidence that our compound is addictive?" Lowell asked.

"Three-dimensional chemical modelling," Wu said.

"That's just hypothetical," Lowell said.

"Actually, we have more than that," Mac said. "Serious problems in some people who have taken it."

"You're a neurosurgeon," Lowell said, now with a sharp edge to his voice. "Why would you know anything about a dietary supplement? Shouldn't you be operating on brains?"

"I see you've done your homework about my vocation," Mac said, "but I have more experience with people taking NoFear than I want to have. I've treated the results of their foolish actions, tried to put them back together after they've jumped off buildings or attempted physical acts beyond human capacity with no concern for consequences."

Lowell's tanned complexion turned red, and his tone became more hostile. "Our preparation is effective and safe. Millions of Americans swear by it. You can't argue with our success."

"But I'm certain that—" Wu protested.

Lowell looked at his watch and stood. "I'm sorry I have another meeting. Thank you so much for taking the time to stop by today. My assistant will see you out."

"Wow! Talk about a stonewall," Wu said as they left the building.

"I think they know it's addictive but are still pushing it," Mac said.

"That would be criminal," Wu said. "Like the makers of some narcotics."

"Mr. Thaddeus Lowell is certainly not going to withdraw NoFear voluntarily," Mac said. "I'm going to the FDA."

不怕

CHAPTER TWENTY-THREE

ENCOUNTER AT THE FDA

FOOD AND DRUG ADMINISTRATION, SILVER SPRING, MD

Mac made multiple attempts to set up an appointment with the Food and Drug Administration about the dangers of NoFear. After spending hours trying to arrange a meeting with no success, he decided to ask Jim Brogan for help.

Brogan headed the CIA section on international terrorist activity, making his job description far above arranging meetings. Mac thought their long history working together would transcend official titles, and he was right. "Let me get this straight," Brogan said on the Zoom call. "You want me to act as your administrative assistant to set up a meeting for you?"

"If you can," Mac said. "It's not a crazy request. I'm getting nowhere, and this may be more than bureaucratic inefficiency. What if NoFear is being used as a biological weapon in the silent war of international terrorism? The FDA could block its distribution in America."

Brogan laughed. "Good point. Of course, I'll do it even if you're wrong. And I'll do it myself because my juniors will think I'm crazy if I ask them. I'd like to know how hard it is to access other government agencies anyway."

He returned a call later in the day. "It took me hours, but I've arranged a slot two days from now for you to see Susan Fraser. She's the assistant director of the FDA responsible for proprietary compounds. You're welcome, and please let me know what happens."

Mac called Grace Wu at once. "I have an appointment to talk about NoFear with the FDA the day after tomorrow. Would you join me?"

"Wow. You must be somebody famous to get a meeting so quickly. I'd be glad to come with you. I want to see this compound banned in America."

The travel to the FDA central office in Silver Spring went smoothly. Mac and Grace took the air shuttle from Logan to Reagan and taxi to get to Silver Spring, Maryland, a lovely Washington suburb with several government agencies.

As they drove past tree-lined streets and pulled up in front of the Food and Drug Administration Headquarters, Mac noted the Jersey barriers that protected the entrance from vehicular assault. "So sad that federal buildings have this kind of cement blockade. I can't say I blame them, considering some of the attacks on government institutions happening regularly now. Citizens all around the country are becoming more aggressive. That, of course, could be a result of NoFear penetrating more and more of the population."

After they showed their ID's and meeting confirmation at the security kiosk, they had no problem finding Susan Fraser's office on the main floor of the sprawling complex.

The administrative assistant showed them in at exactly eleven a.m., the time of their appointment. Fraser looked up from her desk as Mac and Grace entered her office. She did not rise to greet them. No papers or mementos cluttered her sterile workspace, and her chiseled face, auburn hair pulled back into a bun, and darting eyes, gave Mac the impression of a wary animal. *Probably the skillset needed to maintain a position in this bureaucracy.*

"Dr. MacGregor?" Fraser asked, staring at her computer screen.

"Yes, and this is my colleague Dr. Grace Wu."

"Please take a seat," Fraser said. "I'm told you have important information about a compound called NoFear."

"Yes. Do you know this dietary supplement?"

Fraser's gaze darted around the room. Mac thought she was about to lie. "Never heard of it," she said. "And the FDA doesn't regulate dietary supplements."

"You do have the authority in special circumstances to ban proprietary compounds," Mac said. "We believe this is one of those circumstances."

"Don't tell me what we can and can't do," Fraser said. "What is your evidence against this supplement? It is highly irregular for a single individual to speak out against a specific product."

"Although it's marketed as a dietary supplement, we think NoFear is addictive and dangerous," Mac said. He pulled out a folder of graphs and tried to sound as objective as he could as he showed them one by one. "Since NoFear has been introduced to the American market, the United States has seen a hundred percent increase in deaths from unusual causes, in domestic violence, in traffic rage incidents, in demonstrations that turn violent, and in mass shootings. Many of the participants in these events say that NoFear removed their usual reluctance to participate in such violent behavior."

He closed the folder. "We believe these incidents are a result of NoFear's ability to eliminate anxiety."

"Anything else?' Fraser asked, appearing to be unshaken by these data.

"It binds with the locus coeruleus on structural modelling," Wu said. "That means it's addictive."

"Dr. Wu, I'm sure you understand that you can't predict addiction from a three-dimensional computer model," Fraser replied.

"Perhaps," Mac said, "but our data suggest that people who take this drug have a hard time stopping it and need more and more to get the anti-anxiety effect. Those features qualify it as addictive."

"Many proprietary compounds have occasional adverse side effects," Fraser said. "We don't ban them because of that."

"Ms. Fraser," Mac said, having difficulty understanding why she was so oppositional, "We're talking about deaths of normal people who think they can do insane things, not rashes or nausea. NoFear is an addictive drug with an enormous potential for abuse, available at your local health food store. Do you understand how dangerous this situation is?"

Fraser paused, then said. "I think this does require further investigation. If you email me copies of your slides, I will move your concerns up the ladder to try to get some consensus. The young man at the desk will give you our email as you leave. Thank you for bringing this problem to my attention. Now I must get on."

"What the hell was that?" Grace asked as she and Mac waited for the elevator outside Fraser's office.

"More stonewalling. I expect we're finished at the FDA. Everyone else in the agency will be on the lookout for us now and we won't get another appointment. We're going to have to find another way to stop this drug."

Sitting behind her desk in her office, Susan Fraser stared at the clock for five minutes, then buzzed her assistant. "Have those people from Boston left?"

"Yes. I told them where to send the slides. They asked where the nearest taxi stand was."

Fraser was afraid. She opened her desk drawer and took out two NoFear tablets, swallowing them without water. The idea that she should block any investigation of NoFear had seemed reasonable when Sterling Underwood proposed it two months ago. It was a food additive, not a drug, so he argued she could simply declare it was outside jurisdiction.

Of course, she worried about the Panamanian bank account in her name and the scholarship for her daughter that had followed her agreement with Underwood, but no one had asked questions about NoFear. She needed a secure retirement for herself and good education for her child.

Until today, when MacGregor and his colleague walked in bringing up problems and asking questions. Why was MacGregor so interested in NoFear anyway?

She felt sweat beading on her brow. This was more than she had bargained for. Picking up the phone her contact had given her, she pressed its only number. "Sterling?" she asked.

"I told you not to call unless you had an emergency," the voice replied.

"This is an emergency." She described the conversation between Mac and Grace. "What should I do?"

"Nothing. I will take care of the problem." Underwood hung up.

Fraser decided she would take the rest of the day off.

Mac and Grace had lunch in the cafeteria before they headed back to Reagan Airport. After they left the building, they moved toward the taxi stand, weaving through the Jersey barriers that protected the entrance.

Out of the corner of his eye Mac saw a van heading down the hill toward them. He assumed it would stop as they were entering a crosswalk.

They stepped into the street with another pedestrian ahead of them.

The van continued racing toward them.

Mac stared at the vehicle, realized it had no intention of slowing, and pushed Grace back behind the protection of the Jersey wall, moving beside her.

The van smashed into the cement with an earsplitting *WHACK*, moving the slabs several inches. It then ricocheted, sideswiped the woman who had been ahead of them in the crosswalk, and swerved back onto the street. Screams mingled with screeching tires of the runaway vehicle as it merged with traffic and disappeared.

The whole episode raced by so quickly Mac could hardly understand what had just happened. "You OK?" he asked Grace as he checked for external injuries.

"I think so." Her face looked pale. "I wasn't hit by the van or the barrier when it moved. Thank God you were here, though. Can you imagine what would have happened if I had been in front of the barrier rather than behind it?" She wiggled her fingers and toes and stretched her neck to show she was unharmed.

"I'll be right back," Mac said as security guards streamed out of the FDA building. He ran to the sideswiped woman lying in a pool of blood. Her face was as white as her blouse.

Just under the fringe of her linen skirt, a bone protruded through the skin of her thigh with blood pooling around it. Mac pulled off his tie and knotted it around the leg above the fracture, then pushed a ballpoint pen into the knot and twisted it to create a tourniquet. As he twisted, the bleeding slowed and stopped. The woman lay passive, too much in shock to say or do anything.

The EMT team and police arrived. Emergency techs loaded the woman into an ambulance after complimenting Mac on his quick work to stop the bleeding. A uniformed officer introduced herself as Officer Cortland of Federal Protective Services and showed her badge. She asked Grace and Mac to come with her and ushered them through security.

"First room on the right," the guard said as they passed. "We cleared it for you."

"Thanks," Cortland nodded. She led them into a small minimally furnished room and invited them to take a seat as she pulled out her cell phone. "I'm recording our conversation. Can you state your full name and tell me what happened?"

Mac described the sequence of events, including the frosty reception at the FDA.

"Anything unusual about the vehicle?" Cortland asked.

"No license plates," Mac replied. "Could that have been intentional?"

"You think the van might have been targeting you because of your visit to the FDA to stop NoFear?" Cortland asked. "That's paranoid."

"But what other reason could there be?" Grace said, starting to recover. "The driver didn't even try to stop. Why would he head straight for us?"

"People lose control of their vehicles every day." Courtland turned off the recording and added, "By the way, my son takes NoFear regularly for his social anxiety disorder. It has changed his life."

"We believe it's a dangerous drug," Mac said.

"The government wouldn't let a compound stay on the market if it was dangerous," Cortland said. "Half my friends use it. Thank you for your time. I'll be back in touch if I need any more information." She gestured toward the door, and Mac and Grace exited.

During the flight back to Boston, Grace turned to Mac. "I keep thinking about what happened. We came to the FDA with a major concern about a drug. We were stonewalled and a van tried to run us over as we were leaving. Too much coincidence."

Trying to reassure Grace, Mac answered, "As Officer Courtland said, it was probably just a driver who lost control of his vehicle."

"You know that's bullshit," Grace replied. "Whoever's behind the distribution of NoFear doesn't want us snooping around."

"Do you really think they tried to kill us?" Mac asked.

"Probably not. They just wanted to scare us off. And for me at least, it worked. From now on, I'm going to focus on neuropathology. I suggest you do the same. I don't want you falling out of a high window in some hotel. You're too valuable a friend to lose."

不怕

CHAPTER TWENTY-FOUR

STERLING UNDERWOOD'S PARTY

GEORGETOWN, D.C.

Sterling Underwood III knew the party he was about to host was more than a casual gathering of colleagues. It would begin his targets' road to NoFear addiction, meeting his Russian contact's demands with finesse.

Thus far he had done a great job to protect NoFear. He felt especially good about the way he had arranged the van to scare Duncan MacGregor and his friend when they left the FDA building. He hoped they had the sense to stop nosing around so he wouldn't have to do anything more extreme.

To get ready for the party, Underwood inspected each of the ground floor rooms of his Georgetown townhouse. Reception hallway, living room, dining room, library—their burnished wood floors, elegant Georgian furniture, and polished light fixtures and chandeliers shone in the light of an early evening.

He used his white-gloved right hand to wipe the surface of each piece of furniture, an ancient maneuver but one that worked for him. He noted no streaks of dust. With pride, he noted to self that he managed an immaculate house even without his wife.

He didn't miss her. She never could accept his sexual preference for other men.

Given the circumstances, he had created a great life for himself without her. His lobbying paid well, and the naturopathic dietary supplements he represented were an honorable product. There was the slight matter of foreign influence on his decision-making, but his contacts assured him that would never be evident.

The doorbell interrupted his self-congratulation. Underwood welcomed the Minority Leader of the House as the first guest, offering him a radiant smile and a glass of champagne.

"I brought my daughter Sharon," the congressman said. "Wifely duties kept Barbara at home at the last minute. Sharon's a first-year student at Boston University. She's taking a course on the history of American architecture, and I thought she should see what a historic Georgetown townhouse looks like while she's on break."

"Champagne for you too, Sharon," Underwood said, passing her a glass. "I'd be delighted to give you a quick tour before the other guests arrive. Mr. Minority Leader, would you substitute as my official greeter while I show your daughter the house?"

"I think I could handle that," the congressman said, pulling out his iPhone and beginning to read texts as he stood by the door.

Underwood enjoyed showing off his home. Delicate white crown moldings contrasted with pewter-colored walls and oil paintings of distinguished men and outdoor scenes of the late nineteenth century. Antique furniture sat on thick Persian rugs.

"How do you like college so far?" he asked his young guest.

"OK. Sometimes I'm a little overwhelmed."

"Too much schoolwork?"

"Not so much that," Sharon said. "It's all the new people to meet and the academic competition. It's fierce!"

"I'm sure you'll get used to the pressure," Underwood said as they entered his study with its view over P Street. "A big university like BU can be a tough place." He looked out the window to see several guests entering the house.

"Exactly," Sharon said. "And I get so anxious about everything."

"I understand." Underwood pointed to several framed certificates on the wall. "While I was getting these diplomas, I was terrified most of the time. I finally learned to take care of myself with dietary supplements."

"I thought supplements were just glorified vitamins."

"Not at all. That's why I'm a spokesperson for naturopathic products on Capitol Hill. I know they can make a real difference."

He extracted a NoFear starter pack from his pocket and slipped it to Sharon. "Here's my latest find. It might help you deal with stress. I wish it had been available when I was in college."

"What is it?"

"Lessens anxiety, lets you sleep better, makes life a little easier," he said with a smile. "Take this packet and try it for a week. What have you got to lose?"

He turned away. "But enough lecturing. I should get back to my host duties. Look around all you want. I hope the supplement works for you. Here's my card if you need anything."

"Thanks. I may just try it," Sharon said,

Underwood rushed down the staircase to welcome a man whose face was known to millions. "Great that you could find the time to drop in," he said to Tyler Mendax, host of the most-watched infotainment hour on Right TV. "I'm delighted to see you. But can I speak with you privately for a moment?"

"After a double scotch, maybe," Mendax said. "The fall-out from the election is painful. The failed president still wants us to believe he won even though he lost both the popular and electoral vote."

"That could be a devastating problem for someone in your position." Underwood smiled and handed Mendax a double scotch, steering him to the balcony on the upstairs floor. As they stood looking over the beautifully kept houses of P Street, Underwood said, "I thought you should know about a change the Right TV owners are planning to make in the broadcast schedule."

"What change?" Mendax asked, suddenly appearing wary.

"They're going to move your show to the afternoon."

"Excuse me?" Underwood could almost see Mendax's heart pounding beneath the bespoke blue suit. Of course he would be worrying about airwave dominance.

"They're giving up on your bumbling ex-president," Underwood continued. "They think he's too divisive for the country. And as part of the process, they're taking away your bully pulpit. You support him too much."

"No f'ing way," Mendax said. "Where did you hear that? The network's not going to screw me. I'm their most valuable player."

"Doesn't matter where I heard it. Trust me that it's a

reliable source, but I obviously can't tell you who it is. Check it out. Just telling you as a friend. And by the way, if you ever need anything to calm your nerves, try this dietary supplement. It did wonders for me." He slipped a NoFear packet into Mendax's suit pocket.

"Interesting, but I don't believe a word of it," Mendax said, not removing the gift Underwood had slipped him. "I'm the poster child for the network and bring in more viewers than anyone else."

"Check it out for yourself. Why don't we have lunch in a month and follow up? I'll set a date and come to you in New York."

Underwood navigated back to the foyer just in time to see Theodore Tilson, Chief Justice of the Supreme Court, appear at the front door.

"I can only stay for a few minutes" Tilson said.

"I'm so pleased you decided to honor us here even for a second," Underwood said as he guided Tilson to an unoccupied corner of the living room. By this time, clusters of five to ten partygoers had formed in each room.

"I completely understand your distress at the bad press the Court is getting," Underwood said in a confidential tone. "Who would expect such a backlash?"

"It's not only that. We anticipated pushback as soon as the newly seated justices decided to overturn Roe v. Wade. What really makes me angry is the information being revealed about possible financial influence on some of our Justices. After all, we're the Supreme Court. We don't answer to anyone."

Tilson took a glass of champagne with the comment. "Don't you have anything stronger? Anyway, there's one reporter named Daniel Silverman who even has had the balls to target me. Stupid bastard." Tilson downed the champagne in one swallow. "I should be going. Forget everything I just said."

"You must feel terrible about an unwarranted attack like that," Underwood said, putting a hand on Tilson's shoulder to keep him in the conversation. "Polls show confidence in the Supreme Court is low, but you can never trust polls. Listen, I've recently found a dietary supplement helpful in dealing with my own anxiety." He handed a box of NoFear to the justice. "As one anxious man to another, try it for a couple of days. It's not a drug, so you don't have to worry about prescription issues. And it works. I know dozens of people who swear by it. I can get it for you without you having to step out of your house."

"I don't need any pills to face the day," Tilson said, slipping the package into his jacket.

"It's just a dietary supplement, but it will make you feel so much better," Underwood replied. "And good luck with the press."

Tilson excused himself. Underwood mingled, luxuriating in overheard compliments on the quality of the food and social status of the guests. He watched his invitees hover around the quinoa, kale salad and gluten-free offerings, cluster around the carving station with roast beef and turkey, or dive into the cascade of shrimp, oyster, and ceviche.

His party was a social success. More important, it accomplished his objectives. *All targets engaged. My work tonight is done.*

不怕

CHAPTER TWENTY-FIVE

EFFECTS OF NOFEAR: TYLER MENDAX

RIGHT TV STUDIOS, MANHATTAN

Tyler Mendax began taking NoFear regularly after Underwood's party. Armed with the supplement and Underwood's information, he confronted the media company's administration and received a long-term contract. The contract plus the effects of NoFear made him fearless in the topics he presented and the positions they promoted. Now he was not so sure that was wise.

He did remain a COVID-19 denier, and today wanted to discredit the concept of Long COVID. He had invited Harbor Hospital, the leading hospital in the country, to provide two experts to discuss the condition. The Chief Medical Officer had selected Kathleen Green, a pulmonologist with expertise in lung infections, and Dr. Duncan MacGregor, who had personal experience with COVID. "Thanks for the opportunity to have our people talk," Brian Cook had said to Mendax. "It's great publicity for the hospital and perfect for our outreach program."

Too bad the poor guy didn't know what was going to happen to his so-called experts, Mendax thought as he hung up the phone. *They will be made to look like fools.*

The afternoon of the planned appearance, Mac squirmed in the faux-leather chairs of Right TV studios as the make-up artist prepared him for the interview. He perspired not only from the lights. Three years before, he had occupied the same chair before talking with Right TV personality Melody Swift about his COVID experiences in Wuhan China. A persistent COVID denier, Swift had gone on to a terrible death from the virus. The memory continued to haunt Mac.

"Why are we here?" Green whispered to Mac as the make-up artist finished. "I've watched Mendax's shows in the past. He has no interest in truth. He'll just use us to spread his crazy opinion that COVID doesn't exist. I should have told Brian Cook to shove it when he asked me to do this."

Mendax himself stuck his head in the door and flashed his famous smile before Mac could answer. "Nice to have you docs with us tonight. Long COVID is the health buzz of the month. Half the fun will be how you respond to tricky questions. Of course, I can't tell you what they are. Good luck!" He gave a mock salute and disappeared.

Ten minutes later, the two sat across a table from Mendax in a small studio familiar to millions of viewers. Camera operators moved in and around the space and a dozen assistants lurked in the shadows behind the cameras.

Mendax began the interview with a disarming smile and extravagant introduction of the two Harbor Hospital physicians. He knew this was a prelude to making them look foolish. By using Brian Cook as his conduit, he had forced two serious experts to put themselves in harm's way.

"Thank you for talking-with us about what the CDC calls *long COVID*," Mendax said. "Dr. Green, can you tell us what its symptoms are supposed to be?"

"People who have recovered from COVID, even mild

cases, may show shortness of breath, loss of smell, mental fog, and general fatigue months after their original infection," Green said.

"Doctor MacGregor, you claim you had severe COVID. After that, have you noticed any of the problems Dr. Green listed?"

"No, but—"

"That's what I thought," Mendax interrupted. "You got extremely sick but have never had later symptoms. Just shows the CDC doesn't know what it's talking about—"

Mac interrupted. "Long COVID is not a hoax. An alarming number of patients who got infected, especially those who weren't immunized—"

"Whoa," Mendax said, not smiling now. "I do the interrupting here. Does everyone who gets tired have Long COVID?" He turned to the camera. "And mental fog? I think mental fog affects a lot of people, especially Democrats today." He laughed his signature laugh.

"Long COVID is a serious problem," Green said. "The virus leaves behind damage to kidney, lungs, and brain, and probably other organs too."

"Don't you think this is another example of Democrats trying to make—" Mendax paused as if he had lost his train of thought. He frowned and stopped speaking.

Mac stared as Mendax stiffened in his chair. His arms and leg began to twitch. "Call 911 and shut down the cameras," Mac shouted, racing toward his host as he realized this was a seizure. Right TV employees rushed to the desk as Mac lowered Mendax to the floor, loosening the TV star's tie and collar to be sure breathing would be unimpeded.

"What should we do?" the producer of the show asked with eyelids wide.

"Wait for the EMT's," Mac said. "The seizure will pass."

Two minutes later, Mendax stopped shaking, lay unresponsive, then opened his eyes. Mac remained beside him, making sure pulse and respiration were OK.

Mendax tried to sit up, looked around with a wild expression. "What's going on?"

"Take it easy," Mac said, gently holding him down. "You had a seizure."

"A seizure? Tyler Mendax does not have seizures." He lapsed into unconsciousness.

The EMT's arrived shortly after that to provide transport to the hospital.

Mac stayed long enough to confirm everyone was all right after this disaster. As it was now late in the day, he arranged to meet Dr. Green the next morning at the Moynihan Acela terminal to take the train back to Boston.

Shortly after he returned to his hotel, he got a call from his thirteen-year-old daughter Maggie. "Daddy, Daddy. You're famous again."

"What do you mean?"

"You helped Tyler Mendax when he had a seizure."

"How do you know that?"

"TikTok. Somebody posted a video of you treating him. I'm so proud you're my dad."

Still shaken by the events but chuffed by his daughter's praise, Mac answered a second call without giving it much thought. It was from Tyler Mendax's security guard, asking Mac to visit the hospital before he left the city in the morning.

Mac was not sure at all he wanted to comply. He said he would try, then called Lauren and spoke with her and the family. He described the events of the interview and asked them whether he should visit Mendax. The vote was three to zero in favor of making the visit.

As he arrived at Mendax's hospital room the next

morning, he marveled at how bad the Right TV host looked. Disheveled hair, a face furrowed with anxiety...

"I asked you to come here because you're a brain guy and you saw everything," Mendax said. "I want to understand what happened to me yesterday."

"You had a seizure. Haven't your doctors done tests and spoken with you about them?"

"Of course. I've been up all night getting imaged and poked. MRI. Brain waves. Blood and urine tests. No one sees anything wrong. I wanted to ask you something off the record. You and I both know a hospital leaks confidential information like a sieve. I'm counting on you to keep this question a secret."

Mac wondered whether he was about to hear that Mendax had a serious cocaine or methamphetamine habit.

"I don't do drugs," Mendax continued, as if he had read Mac's mind, "but there is a dietary supplement I've used for months. I stopped it a couple of days ago."

Mac's eyelids narrowed. "What supplement?"

"NoFear. A guy convinced me to try it for anxiety. It worked, but I needed more and more to level me out. Have you ever heard of it?"

"Yes," Mac said, remembering the boy who died in the Bosporus, the girl he had to operate on because she jumped from a stairway, and Sophie Grainger who also had seizures when she withdrew from NoFear.

"Could my seizure have anything to do with stopping it?"

"Yes. I do believe stopping NoFear suddenly can cause a seizure," Mac said.

"Then why the hell isn't it being regulated by the FDA? And why are half the people in Washington taking it?"

"I don't know. Who supplies it for you?"

Mendax paused. "Sterling Underwood, a lobbyist for dietary supplements. Very influential behind the scenes in Congress and the Supreme Court."

"Would you consider Underwood your dealer?"

"Not exactly. You can get NoFear in any health food store, but Underwood had high potency pills that worked much better than the stuff in health stores. Besides, he was very discreet. I came to rely on him."

"Why did you stop?"

"I think I was becoming addicted, and I was doing stupid things like inviting more and more extreme Make American Right Again converts on my show. Part of that was because Underwood pressured me, but I also thought I could do whatever I wanted with impunity. NoFear is named appropriately. It makes you unafraid of the consequences of your actions. I made bad decisions under its influence."

He stared at Mac. "Who knows how many people Underwood convinced to take this supplement? Maybe that's why the MARA group is so out of control. That stuff needs to be taken off the market."

"I don't suppose you'd be willing to say that on air?" Mac said.

"Probably not," Mendax said. "I think most of the camera crew takes it, and I expect the majority of my viewers do as well. In my profession, you have to be very careful about what you say so you'll keep your viewers happy. Thanks for coming by. I'm going to stay off that drug now that I've withdrawn."

不怕

CHAPTER TWENTY-SIX

EFFECTS OF NOFEAR: THEODORE TILSON

HOME OF SUPREME COURT JUSTICE THEODORE TILSON, POOLESVILLE, MD

"Can you turn that damn TV off?" Justice Theodore Tilson shouted to his wife from his dressing room. Completing the Windsor knot on his Hermes tie, he marched into her bedroom to emphasize his request.

Jocelyn was still in bed, propped up on pillows, sipping coffee provided by their housekeeper. "But darling," she said, flashing the smile that had become her trademark, "you're all the news this morning. The impeachment trial of a Supreme Court justice is a big deal." She added with a smirk and sarcastic tone, "I just hope you've taken your NoFear today."

"Leave it alone," Tilson shouted, feeling his blood pressure begin to rise. "It's because of you those congressional bastards put me on trial."

His wife bristled. "Don't blame your troubles on me. We agree about the elections and the need to put Republicans back in power. You're just too chicken to say it out loud. And don't forget all those little perks we've gotten from your backers."

She swung her plus size body out of bed and grabbed a bathrobe from the chair. Standing face to face with her husband and not smiling now, she added "And anyway, you and your court are doing more to disrupt the country than I ever could."

"What do you mean by that?" Tilson said, eyelids narrowing.

"Reversing abortion law. Supporting voting restrictions. Liberalizing gun laws. Giving more power to big corporations. Your court might be singlehandedly tanking the United States as we know it. Which I am completely in favor of." She moved to the window. "If you need proof, just look at those demonstrators outside our house."

"They're a bunch of misguided liberals who believe they can kill babies without consequences," Tilson snorted. "I have no respect for them or their values. And that prick Silverman! He keeps digging up dirt on me because he thinks he'll get a Pulitzer. If we could get rid of him, things would be far more manageable."

"Don't worry about it," Jocelyn said, her smile returning. "You know the Democrats don't have enough senate votes to bring any impeachment to conclusion. Just follow our former president's lead, consider it a badge of honor to be so important in the American system as to be impeached, and put up with the crap you'll have to take for the next few days." She crawled back into bed.

"You think it's that easy on a person with my standing?" Tilson said, turning as he stormed out. "These reporters and demonstrators are nobodies, but they make daily life intolerable. The same is true for Congress. Insane leftists trying to destroy our country. The situation makes my blood boil."

Tilson shook his fist at the demonstrators gathered outside his house and fumed as he strode back to his own bedroom. He finished dressing, strapping his shoulder holster and Smith & Wesson model 69 combat magnum against his left armpit. He was glad he had helped the court strike down Washington's restrictive handgun law in *D.C. v. Heller* fourteen years ago. Since then, he always carried a firearm when he was outside the house or Supreme Court building. It was an insurance policy. He never knew what crazy onlookers might attack him on the way to work.

He popped two NoFear tablets into his mouth.

When he stepped out the front door to face the crowd around his house, his heart began to pound and blood pressure rose even further. His immaculate front lawn dotted with saucer magnolias and dogwood trees was cordoned off with yellow "Do Not Cross" tape. He could see news teams from major network waiting like vultures behind the roped-off area. A motley gathering filled the street behind the news cameras, waiting for their prey.

"Impeach Tilson, impeach Tilson!" The repeated chant of the demonstrators contaminated his quiet Maryland neighborhood. Their placards and scruffy appearance, including the occasional waft of marijuana, violated the sanctity of his home.

He felt rage building inside him, paused to stare at the crowd confronting him.

Jocelyn and he had been good neighbors, observing Halloween, Christmas, and Easter with appropriate celebrations. He had always tried to keep his political views to himself, but his wife had a different approach. She was loud and argumentative. That's where things got messy. Jocelyn's public misbehavior got him into trouble.

Sterling Underwood turned out to be his savior by suggesting NoFear to quell anxiety. Since then, that so-called dietary supplement had made life much more tolerable.

Jocelyn started to take NoFear too, and after that became increasingly obstreperous. Her brazen comments about election fraud landed him in his present impeachment morass for alleged conflict of interest. Taking a page from her book, he vigorously denied any conflict.

Now it was almost a contest to see which of them would do the stupider thing. Even today, starting an impeachment trial, part of him thought. *Just say what you want and to hell with them all.*

He returned abruptly to the world in front of him. Daniel Silverman, the little shit of a reporter who had become his nemesis, had somehow slipped through the restraining line and blocked his path. A television camera hung over Silverman's left shoulder like a grotesque eye.

"Justice Tilson," Silverman began to shout, "as the first Supreme Court Justice to undergo an impeachment trial since 1805, do you have any comments?"

How had this man breached his property to confront him? Tilson tried to search beyond the crowd for the U.S. Marshal escort waiting for him in the car, who perhaps had not seen what was happening. He sped up his pace toward the parked vehicle.

"Back then," Silverman followed him, "Samuel Chase's impeachment was blocked by the senate. Do you think you will be so lucky, or will the senators today realize that you have failed in your duty as a Supreme Court Justice?"

Where is the police protection I need? Tilson thought as he moved toward his waiting car.

A sudden surge of the crowd broke the restraints and poured reporters and demonstrators onto his front lawn.

Tilson panicked. *Was this turning into a mob? Was lynching next?* With his vision and thinking distorted by the NoFear he had taken so regularly, Tilson felt his blood simmer with rage against these plebians who surrounded him. He also had to admit that a sense of growing panic poked into his consciousness despite his anti-anxiety pill. *What if this demonstration got out of hand? And where is the Marshall who's supposed to be protecting me?*

"Do you think your wife will go to prison because of her seditious beliefs?" Silverman would just not let up as he raced beside him "And what about your children? Are they embarrassed by their parents' treachery?"

Stretched to the breaking point, Tilson felt his panic dissipate. The situation had gone far enough. He realized that no matter what the outcome, the trial that was about to start would bring disgrace. He decided what he had to do, and he was not afraid to do it.

This man, this cockroach in front of him, had hounded and humiliated him for years. A reporter attacking a Supreme Court justice? No system should allow such a thing. And the attack would continue until his wife and children were destroyed.

Tilson reached into his vest for his Smith & Wesson. Cool now, not afraid of what would follow, he drew the pistol, aimed at Silverman's thick glasses, and fired.

His antagonist dropped like a stone to the sidewalk. Screams as the crowd realized what had happened made him realize what he had done. The previously invisible U.S. Marshal ran from the car and the news teams raced toward him.

Tilson turned the pistol towards his own forehead and pulled the trigger.

不怕

CHAPTER TWENTY-SEVEN

REACTION

BROOKLINE, MA

Mac could not believe what he was seeing on the television screen. He and Lauren were having a rare morning together in their Brookline home and had just heard the news that a Supreme Court justice had killed a reporter and then himself. Sun streamed through the window, but the TV images brought only darkness to Mac's soul.

The news cameras showed the chaotic scene around Justice Tilson's house. The crowds had swelled to mob size. Fights broke out among the demonstrators every few minutes. One reporter asked a woman being led away in handcuffs why she had assaulted a police officer even though she knew she would be arrested. "I used to be afraid of standing up for what I believe," she said. "Now I'm afraid of nothing."

In one corner, a man in combat gear displaying a paramilitary shoulder patch was approached by a female reporter. "Why are you here in uniform?" she asked.

"I came over when I heard that reporter was shot," he said. "I'm going to kick ass if necessary. He deserved what he got, and no one is going to convince me of anything different. The press is part of the whole conspiracy against us."

"You think Justice Tilson did the right thing?"

"Shooting the reporter? Of course. When elections are being stolen and our country is taken over by communists, you have to stand up for what you believe. That jerk reporter was going after one of the guys on the Supreme Court who's actually on our side."

"Do you think Tilson was in favor of violence?"

The man stared at his interviewer. "Are you trying to mix me up and get me to say something that sounds bad? Just remember, you're a reporter too. When we take over this country, people like you better watch your back." He turned and walked away.

"What is our country coming to?" Lauren asked as the camera switched scenes. "It's as if violent support of any crazy position has become the norm. Extremists have—"

Loud chanting from the television screen interrupted her. A cluster of people holding Make America Right Again banners marched toward the crowd. "Stop the socialists," they shouted, "return our country to us."

"And just listen to what the Chinese and Russian bots are spreading on social media," Lauren continuing, reading from her smart phone.

Another plot by Antifa.

Tilson thought the gun was loaded with blanks.

Tilson was forced by Democrats to do this as punishment for his stance on abortion.

She held up her phone displaying a TikTok post. The face of a white male filled the screen. Under the heading *Supreme Court Shooting Solved*, the narrator claimed. "I have definite evidence that the man firing the shot was a body double for Tilson, not the justice himself. The murder-suicide was a plot by the left wing to disrupt the American legal system so they could pack the Supreme Court and take over the country. They are holding Tilson hostage even now. We must find and save him."

After that, a second video message appeared, delivered by an attractive white woman. "Here's breaking news. Tilson and the reporter involved were having a secret gay affair. That's why the justice shot the man. A crime of passion."

Mac shook his head at the sea of deliberate misinformation that swamped this and any other newsworthy event. He expected that China and Russia had developed ways of infiltrating social media to spread lies, raise doubts, and normalize outrageous behavior. The realization made him cosmically depressed, since he knew many Chinese and Russian neurosurgeons who were, as his mother used to say, "Good people."

Lauren broke into his train of thought. "Mac, this is insane. What makes the demonstrators so fearless? Why on earth would a Supreme Court justice think he should shoot a reporter?"

The memory of Hassan leaping into the Bosporus flashed through Mac's mind.

"I have an idea," he said, realizing that the reckless action he had just seen was exactly what NoFear did to its victims. Could its use have penetrated all the way to the Supreme Court? "Lauren, would you please excuse me? I want to call Jim Brogan."

Lauren nodded and left.

Brogan answered on the third ring. Their long and productive collaboration allowed immediate response to each other's calls.

"What's up, Mac?" Brogan asked. "We're busy sorting out this Supreme Court mess."

"That's what I called about, Jim. I'm sure the investigators have post-mortem samples of Tilson's blood for drug analysis. Can you be sure they do a specific search for NoFear? This looks to me like exactly the kind of event that compound can produce."

Three days later, Mac's hunch about NoFear was confirmed when the New York Times ran the headline, "Tilson's death linked to dietary supplement." The article described the story of NoFear, the attempt by several doctors including Mac to get the FDA to withdraw it, and the opposition that followed. It particularly emphasized the inadequate regulation of dietary supplements, which now formed a multi-billion-dollar industry that had almost no oversight. Media support of 'natural' compounds instead of rigorously tested medication to treat medical problems played a large part in this dangerous situation. So, too, did the extensive army of Washington lobbyists whose jobs were funded by the dietary supplement companies.

The report continued with the fact that high concentrations of NoFear were found in Tilson's body. In an exclusive Times interview, Tilson's wife confirmed that he had been taking up to six pills a day of the supplement. "There's been a lot of trouble around the court these last few years," she said, "and NoFear helped him move forward on the path he wanted."

Maybe a murder by a Supreme Court Justice will be what it takes to prompt a congressional investigation into NoFear, Mac thought, immediately upset by his own callousness.

不怕

CHAPTER TWENTY-EIGHT

EFFECTS OF NOFEAR: SHARON

BROOKLINE, MA

During the COVID-19 pandemic, Lauren MacGregor had reorganized a corner of the guest bedroom as her workspace. After that she continued to use the desk, file cabinet, and computer as an office for her never-ending tasks as a teacher.

On a cloudy October morning, the jangle of the doorbell startled her from work. She checked her daily log and confirmed that she expected no deliveries or visitors. After a quick glance in the mirror, she descended the stairway to the front door.

A girl about nineteen with dirty hair, rumpled clothes, and the unmistakable odor of urine, slouched in the doorway. She seemed shaky and picked at healing scabs on her left forearm as she spoke.

"Do you remember me, Mrs. MacGregor?" the girl asked, eyes downcast.

Lauren stood, racked her brain to make the connection she needed, and lifted the girl's head. "Sharon?" she asked. "Sharon Dunegan?" She remembered the bright, attractive young woman she had known in last year's graduating class.

"That's me," Sharon said, then looked at the floor. "I'm in trouble."

"Come in," Lauren said, stepping away from the doorway and wondering how this involved her. She led Sharon to the conservatory, where the smell of orange blossoms filled the air, and beckoned her to sit. "Can I get you something to eat or drink?" she asked.

"No. Not eating much these days," Sharon muttered, and began to cry.

Lauren took one hand in hers. "What's happened? How did you get into this state?"

"Remember I went to Boston University after I graduated? I wanted to get away from my crazy family. You were a big factor—my favorite teacher. You said I could get back in touch with you any time. Here I am."

"I remember," Lauren said, trying to convey as much sympathy as she could, "and I'm going to get you something to eat." She moved to the kitchen and returned with a platter of cookies and two cups of English Breakfast tea.

Sharon added several spoons of sugar before sipping her tea. Her hands were shaking as she lifted the cup and carefully replaced it on the saucer. "I got so anxious I couldn't decide what courses to take. Mom said try several and decide which ones you like, but at BU that's like saying swim in a hurricane. There are hundreds of options. My dad was no help either. Told me to use my stupid advisers. I think he just wanted to focus his time backing that loser ex-president."

"That still doesn't explain what got you into this state, Sharon. What else?"

"Can I trust you?" Sharon looked at Lauren with a sideways glance.

"To do what?" Lauren sat back.

"Not to tell my parents. To be on my side."

"Why? What's going on?'

"I've just been kicked out of summer school and my apartment," Sharon blurted out. "Could I hang here for a couple of days until I get myself together?"

Lauren stiffened. *What was this leading to?* She looked at Sharon's arms, saw needle scars on the right forearm, and said, "I'll have to talk with my husband, but you're welcome to stay tonight." Taking Sharon to the guest room, she handed her a towel and bathrobe and took the dirty clothes to wash. "Why don't you take a shower and rest until dinner time? You have a couple of hours to relax."

When she checked half an hour later, Sharon was soundly asleep on the guestroom bed.

Lauren called Mac. "Would you be willing to have a houseguest for a few days?"

"Whose name would be...?"

"Sharon Dunegan. I taught her two years ago. She's the daughter of the House Minority Leader."

"Any special reason you invited her to stay with us? We've never invited one of your former students to spend the night before,"

"She's having a tough time," Lauren said. "Maybe we can discuss it tonight?"

"Sure, go ahead."

In baggy cotton pants and an oversize button-down shirt borrowed from Lauren, Sharon looked like a normal exhausted teenager when she joined the family for dinner. Lauren introduced her to Maggie and Peter as a former student who was back in Boston for a few days working on a college project. Lauren would be helping her.

Sharon ate tentatively, as though reluctant to add food

to her stomach. Mac and Lauren led the conversation, mainly focusing on their own college experiences, avoiding any personal questions for Sharon. Maggie and Peter spoke only occasionally and with great restraint. They seemed to sense that something tense was happening and asked to be excused as soon as they finished eating.

After dinner, Lauren asked Sharon to accompany them to the conservatory, which they used as a space for unfettered conversation. Fruit trees, fragrant plants, subdued lighting, and informal furniture provided visual and olfactory comfort.

"I told Mac a little of what's happened to you," 'Lauren began. "Can you help us fill in the rest?"

"You have to promise not to tell my parents," Sharon began, fidgeting with her hands.

"I felt I couldn't keep up at BU. I failed two courses and was put on probation. I had to take summer courses to make up the classes I bombed. My parents agreed to fund them."

She stood and began to pace. "At my break, I went back to see my parents for a week. A man called Sterling Underwood gave me some pills at a party my dad took me to. He claimed they were a dietary supplement without any side effects and would help me study." She stopped and stared at her hands. "I wish I hadn't listened to him."

"The name of the pills?" Mac asked, apprehensive now.

"NoFear. I don't have any to show you."

"And the next thing that happened?" he asked.

"I came back to Boston and rented a studio near methadone mile. I acted out in my classes, didn't finish homework, criticized my teachers, thought I was far superior to anyone else in the class. All this time I was popping NoFear pills like crazy."

"Were you worried about what might happen in the end?" Lauren asked.

Sharon shook her head. "I didn't care about anything, did vodka shots for a while, then drugs. Pretty soon no money or friends or food. Stopped going to classes and tried to find work."

"All this in one summer?" Mac asked.

Sharon nodded. "Actually, only five weeks."

She began to sob. Lauren took her hand as she sniveled and shook. After a few minutes she seemed to pull herself together. "I tried waitressing and couldn't stand the entitled customers. I also hated the schedule. At Sterling's suggestion, I tried dating for money."

Lauren looked at Mac and shook her head as blood chilled in her veins.

"That was a disaster." Sharon continued. "I got beaten up a couple of times."

She touched an old bruise on her cheek as silence enveloped the room.

"What happened next?" Mac asked softly, wondering how bad this story would get.

Sharon looked up, wiped her eyes. "I decided I had to get clean. I stopped everything, including NoFear. Decided I would not talk with that bastard Underwood."

"Did you ask for medical help?" Mac asked. "Boston Medical Center has resources to help young people in your situation."

"I didn't trust anyone. I did it alone."

"And?" Mac asked.

"I almost died. Spent days on my bed sweating and twisting. Had hallucinations and maybe seizures. I blacked out and woke up with sore muscles. All that ended just two days ago."

She shuddered and looked into the distance as if she could see herself back then.

Lauren and Mac waited, silent.

"My landlord kicked me out yesterday because I hadn't paid my rent for weeks. I couldn't go to my parents. They don't care and my dad controls mom and everybody else. I decided to turn to you." She looked at Lauren. "Did I mention you were my favorite teacher?"

"What do you want to do now?" Lauren asked.

"Get back on my feet and return to school without losing the rest of the semester. And I don't want my parents to know about any of this."

"When was the last time you talked with them?" Lauren asked.

"Two weeks ago."

"You should call them to let them know you're OK. I expect they're worried."

Sharon sat up very straight and a cold stare replaced her tears. "You have to promise me you won't tell them about the stuff I just told you."

"Let's talk about it in the morning," Mac said, looking at his watch. "It's past my bedtime and I'm sure you're still pretty tired."

"OK," Sharon said. "I couldn't stand the fallout if newspapers got hold of this story."

Lauren hung Sharon's clean clothes in the guest room closet. "I'm glad you came to see me, Sharon," she said. "You've had a very difficult summer. Try to get some rest."

In bed, Lauren asked Mac what to do. "Can you imagine how we would feel if some unknown persons were taking in Maggie after a story like Sharon's? It's just awful."

"Frankly, I can't imagine it," he said, "But at some point, her folks need to know."

Lauren thought she heard someone in the hall but found no one when she got up to look. She lay awake staring at the ceiling for an hour before getting to sleep.

Lauren woke the next morning to Maggie tugging on her pillow. Half opening her eyes, she looked at the clock. It was six a.m.

"Mom! Mom! Sharon's gone!" Maggie said.

"I'm sure she's just downstairs getting breakfast," Lauren said.

"No, I've looked everywhere. And her clothes are gone too."

Lauren searched the empty guest room, bathroom, and kitchen with Maggie. "Maybe she just went for a morning walk?" Maggie asked.

"Perhaps," Lauren said. When she found her open purse in the hall with her credit cards and a hundred dollars cash missing, she realized Sharon had probably disappeared for good.

不怕

CHAPTER TWENTY-NINE

THE NOFEAR CONGRESSIONAL COMMITTEE

BROOKLINE, MA AND WASHINGTON, DC

Blocked in his attempts to get NoFear regulated, Mac decided to pay more attention to his work and family. For a month he focused on surgery, teaching, research, and intentional time with Lauren, Maggie, and Peter.

A Zoom call from Jim Brogan changed all that.

"Mac," Brogan said without introductory niceties, "We've finally been able to get action in Congress on NoFear. Could you testify before a congressional committee next week about its negative effects?"

Mac paused, then asked, "Why me? I'm a surgeon, not a drug expert. Wouldn't someone like Dr. Grace Wu be more appropriate?"

"I ran many names by the organizing committee," Brogan said. "We want *you*. You've seen the effects of this drug first-hand. Who else has tried to rescue a kid who died swimming in dangerous waters after taking the drug? Or has done surgery on a teenager who developed a brain clot because she took NoFear and jumped from a stairway? Also, you have a very impressive curriculum vitae. I mean, two hundred professional publications. We'd have a hard time finding a witness with more credibility."

"How did the committee get formed so fast?" Mac asked, embarrassed by Brogan's compliments.

"I went directly to John Jameson. He's an old friend, but he's changed from a reasonable politician to a Make American Right Again Republican. He still says the last presidential election was stolen."

"So how did you persuade him to investigate NoFear?" Mac got up to pour himself a cup of coffee.

"Claimed the Chinese government is using this compound to destabilize America. Showed him the statistics. The rate of unnecessary deaths in this country has increased more than a hundred percent in the last three months, and it's accelerating. Kids step in front of cars, jump off buildings. They take guns to school and kill teachers. Adults quit their jobs, then come back and kill their coworkers. And in states like Texas, the combination of NoFear and loose gun laws has created an impossible situation."

"Did you mention the TikTok challenge problem as well?" Mac said. "That Chinese App seems to be deliberately stoking dangerous behavior. Yesterday, it challenged Maggie and Peter to hit a teacher or run in front of a car. Fortunately, they didn't comply. Fear of consequences including the wrath of their parents protected them. A few NoFear pills and that protection would have been gone."

"What did you do when you learned about this?"

"Banned TikTok from the house, and we check every couple of days for hidden pills. We've talked to the kids too, and both say no one has offered them anything at school…yet."

"I hope that approach works. There's a lot of peer pressure on kids to take this stuff. TikTok and NoFear are a one-two punch from China. Fortunately, Jameson also has a couple of teenagers. He seemed skeptical at first about an investigation. If

I claimed Russia was behind the epidemic of deaths, I wouldn't have had a chance. The MARA Republicans often side with the Soviets. But with China as the bad guy, Jameson agreed to create an urgent special ad hoc committee to evaluate NoFear. It will meet for five days next week, so we're on a very tight schedule."

"Who else will be testifying?" Mac asked.

"Parents, pharmacologists, lobbyists. But your experience is unique. You've been part of this compound since its early days, and you've examined the brains of users. Can I count on you?"

"I'll have to talk with Lauren and my administrator, but I think so," Mac said. He stared at the screen. A year ago, he would have had nothing to do with persuading congress to ban a drug. Now he realized that this might save more lives than his surgery could in his lifetime.

Brogan was waiting in a limousine when Mac arrived at Reagan Airport. En route to the Capitol, the CIA official provided a brief description of each committee member, summarized what other witnesses had said, and told Mac what to expect. "So far, testimony confirms the drug is effective for anxiety and is widely used."

"That helps our case," Mac said. "The more effective it is, the more it needs to be regulated like a drug."

"Exactly what we hope you'll prove."

Seeing the mall with the Washington Monument, Lincoln Memorial, and Capitol building filled Mac with an unexpected emotion—pride at what America was and had been. There was no need to Make America Right Again. Just give it a chance—its heart was already right as rain.

The Capitol committee room held about a hundred spectators. The wooden benches gave off the aroma of seasoned oak. People of every age, skin shade, and body shape filled the seats. Bright lights illuminated every corner.

"Speakers are in the front row," Brogan whispered as he led Mac to his seat. "Members of the media and government officials sit behind them."

"And the audience?" Mac asked.

"I must admit most are NoFear enthusiates. We had to make that concession to Jameson."

"Who's that speaking now?" Mac asked.

"Sterling Underwood, a lobbyist for dietary supplements. He's an advocate for continuing the status quo."

Mac remembered that Sharon Dunegan had mentioned Sterling Underwood in her story. That must be the person testifying now. He saw a pudgy man with gray hair and a soft rounded face reminiscent of a soft-nosed pig. A genteel southern accent made his speech seem less threatening than the words he spoke.

"There is no reason to change anything," Underwood purred as Brogan and Mac slid into their reserved seats. "NoFear is not a drug. It is merely a dietary supplement. And as you have heard, it is a very effective way of diminishing anxiety. The United States Government has the authority to regulate the content and manufacturing process of such a supplement, but not its use or distribution. No restrictions should be imposed on it any more than ginger ale. The arguments you are going to hear in favor of regulating NoFear come from the big drug companies who want to control everything. Don't let them do it. This is a free country."

He stepped away from the speaker desk and returned to his seat.

"You're next," Brogan said. "Stay cool."

不怕

CHAPTER THIRTY

MAC TESTIFIES IN CONGRESS

WASHINGTON, D.C.

John Jameson, chairperson of the Ad Hoc Committee to Investigate NoFear, was a gray-haired man with eyes that never settled on one object for long. "Dr. MacGregor," he said when Mac stood. "Please take a seat at the microphone. Am I correct that you are a neurosurgeon at Harbor Hospital in Boston?"

"Yes."

"If I may be blunt, why are you here?" Jameson asked. "What does a dietary supplement have to do with neurosurgery?"

Mac heard muffled laughter from the audience, prompting him to answer aggressively. "I've watched a boy drown because he took NoFear and tried to swim against a deadly current, a girl almost die of a skull fracture and brain clot after NoFear made her jump from a stairway. I attended the autopsy of a woman on NoFear who thought she could burn down a building with no repercussions. And of course, I watched, as we all did, the images of a Supreme Court Justice loaded with NoFear kill a reporter. I—"

"But how do you know those events happened because of NoFear?" Jameson interrupted. "Those were probably very sick people to start with. We can't make policy based on single cases like that. May I remind you that NoFear has been demonstrated to be safe over and over again. Many people take it without problems, including my own children. I think some of our committee members swear by it as well." He looked left and right and saw a couple of quiet nods.

"All right," Mac said, raising his voice further. "Let me give you more general examples from the hospital I work in. I sit on the care improvement committee, a group that tries to improve hospital performance. Since NoFear has been easily available, we have experienced a huge uptick in bad decision-making among nurses and physicians. Surgeons undertake operations they have no training for, with terrible results. Malpractice cases have skyrocketed because patients have no patience. Nurses take breaks to finish chart notes rather than take care of patients, or cancel their shifts at the last minute, leaving the hospital understaffed. Trainees don't show up for work and don't care about the consequences of being AWOL. Our hospital life has become chaotic."

The audience buzzed. A few booed.

Mac paused for a moment, then continued. "My wife, who teaches in high school, says the same kind of disruption is happening in the educational system. Teachers hit students who frustrate them. Of course they're fired, and the school ends up understaffed because they leave. In some states, students hit teachers and come back with weapons to kill people. Bus drivers taking young children home drive aggressively and get into serious accidents. Schools are out of control."

"Mr. Chairman, a question," a member of the committee asked.

"The chair recognizes the congresswoman from Massachusetts," Jameson said.

A petit woman rose from her seat. "Thank you, Mr. Chairman, and thank you for coming to speak with us today, Dr. MacGregor."

"I'm glad to do anything that will deal with NoFear," Mac said.

"May I ask what you suggest we do?"

"At the very least," Mac said, "add NoFear to the list of drugs regulated by the Drug Enforcement Agency. It is a habit-forming and dangerous drug and should only be prescribed by doctors, not bought over the counter like candy."

"And at most?" the congresswoman asked.

"Ban NoFear completely. Make it illegal to buy or sell."

Loud boos and hisses filled the room and could not be stopped despite the chairman's demand for order. Finally, a prominent MARA Republican member of the committee asked for time to speak and was granted it by Jameson.

The audience quieted, and the MARA congressman spoke. "Dr. MacGregor, isn't this just another example of you doctors trying to increase control over patients?"

The crowd cheered.

"Have you ever taken NoFear, Dr. MacGregor? Do you know anything about these addictive effects you're talking about."

Shouts from the bystanders.

Yeah

Right on

Stick it to him

"That's like asking if I've ever tried cocaine," Mac said. "No, I've never tried NoFear."

"Well, you might consider it," the MARA congressman

said. "It's helped a lot of voters in my district. If people use it unwisely, that's up to them. In America we call that freedom."

Applause erupted from the audience, forcing Jameson to call for order.

"Like the freedom to take an AK47 and kill school children?" Mac said, feeling the blood pump harder through his body. "The combination of easy-to-get-guns and easy-to get NoFear is particularly deadly. And will you ignore the massive increase in road rage accidents, violent demonstrations, and domestic violence cases everywhere in the country since NoFear was available?"

Jameson cut Mac's mike and said loudly. "Doctor, this is not a committee to evaluate guns and the protection of citizens afforded by our second amendment. I don't believe we need to hear any more. Please step down."

The audience clapped, hooted, pointed, slapped each other on the shoulders, dissolved into disorder despite everything Jameson could try to calm them. Mac could see Underwood smirk and Brogan wave his arms, pointing to the emergency exit.

Mac's head pounded in response to the insanity around him. He walked fast toward the exit, where Brogan covered his departure as a bodyguard would protect a rock star.

They slammed the door behind them as they left the building. Mac leaned against the wall, allowing his racing heart to slow. "I don't think we're going to persuade this committee to do anything," he said. "I'm sorry to have gotten hot under the collar."

"No problem," Brogan said. "I now realize the hearing is a sham to allow the MARA group to say they did an investigation. I wouldn't be surprised if the commotion was planned if anyone dared question freedom to take NoFear.

You just happened to be the chosen target. To get anything done, we'll have to go elsewhere than Congress."

At home later that night, Mac tuned to Right TV, a conservative broadcasting network, to see how they presented the events of the day. In a segment dealing with the NoFear congressional committee, Jameson's face smiled at the camera. "Our committee has almost finished its job," Jameson said. "I can't leak the final report, but I can give you a general idea of our thinking. It comes down to this. An attack on NoFear is an attack on Americans' fundamental right to do what they want. Millions of us take this supplement every day. We did not hear one convincing account of NoFear causing a problem."

Mac stared at the screen in disbelief, then muttered to himself. "A drowned kid, a dead woman, a murdered reporter, a disgraced justice, an increase in violent crimes...Aren't these convincing examples of a problem?" He felt his head throb at the deliberate denial of reality.

He was holding the remote in his hand to cut off the television transmission when the host of this prime-time show said, "Even if there were problems with NoFear, the solution is simple. The answer to bad guys taking NoFear is good guys taking NoFear who stop them. Most of the NoFear addicts are non-white illegals anyway."

Jameson stared into the camera and said, in a comment that had clearly been pre-arranged. "Well said. We are committed to upholding freedom and our fellow Americans' right to choose. We have more important things to worry about than a dietary supplement. Every day in our country, immigrants are replacing legitimate Americans, the government is increasing taxes on the captains of industry who guide our economy, and our southern border is being breached. We're going to focus on those problems and leave dietary supplements for individual choice."

The TV host's face filled the screen for the final comment. "Of course, Democratic socialists want to control everything you do including decide what food you eat. They won't stop until they legislate where you live, who you have as neighbors, who your kids go to school with. They are trying to replace you and me with people you would not want to be seen dead with, people who will vote for them and take this country away from us. We can't let that happen—"

Mac punched the remote and watched the face dissolve into a black screen.

不怕

CHAPTER THIRTY-ONE

WHY NOFEAR SPREADS

BROOKLINE, MA

After his NoFear Congressional Committee testimony, Mac returned to work and home responsibilities, but NoFear kept gnawing at the back of his mind. A month after the Congressional hearing, he called Jim Brogan with an idea he had developed while carrying out an experiment in his brain tumor laboratory.

"Jim, I've been thinking about the similarity between NoFear and a malignant brain tumor."

"I knew I shouldn't have answered this call," Brogan said.

"Hear me out. Glioblastoma, the worst brain tumor I treat, cloaks itself from the body's surveillance mechanisms. It can spread its malignant cells through the brain because the immune system does not recognize it as a threat."

"And what does that have to do with a dietary supplement?"

"NoFear spreads because it hides from regulatory processes normally meant to control such a compound."

"Maybe," Brogan said. "But that's because our surveillance system is broken. Congress is riddled with NoFear users and lawmakers acting as unwitting or deliberate foreign assets."

"You think they're on China's payroll?'

"Don't have to be. They propagate lies spread by TikTok and Chinese social media bots. I expect the direct payoffs go to lobbyists like Sterling Underwood. But how is China's influence in American politics relevant to stopping NoFear?"

"You said China has prohibited the distribution and sale of NoFear within its own borders," Mac said.

"Absolutely. They know it would cause chaos."

"Don't you think their attempts to limit it will fail, just as ours have? There's so much social and physical interchange with other countries that NoFear's bound to infiltrate China too. American defense mechanisms may be inadequate, but like a malignant brain tumor, this drug will inevitably boomerang back into the People's Republic of China."

"Why do you think that? China is repressive and closed now," Brogan said.

"Back in the early twentieth century, aggressive brain surgeons sometimes removed half a patient's brain to stop the progression of glioblastoma. They thought they could keep it from moving from one side of the brain to the other."

"And?" Brogan asked.

"The tumor appeared in the good half of the brain a few weeks after the surgery and went on to kill the patient just as if no surgery had been done."

"So, what are you suggesting?"

"We wait until China feels the impact of the inevitable infiltration of NoFear, then try to broker a collaborative deal to block it worldwide."

"That's a crazy idea," Brogan said. "First, China is more repressive than we are. There's a much higher probability they can shut down drug infiltration than there is with us."

"But like a malignant glial cell, this compound can escape detection. Its producers slip by the usual surveillance and control mechanisms."

Brogan continued, ignoring Mac's comment. "Second, there's little chance China would acknowledge the spread of NoFear to the outside world even if it were occurring within its borders. Look what China did during the early days of COVID-19, when it refused to acknowledge the beginning of a world crisis."

"They would keep up the lie unless they realize it would destroy their social fabric too," Mac said.

"Third, even if they acknowledged it, the possibility of getting a joint effort by the United States and China to control anything is small."

"Don't be such a pessimist," Mac said. "One event at a time. All I suggest right now is that your Chinese contacts watch out for the kind of insane events occurring in China that we've noted with NoFear in this country. You might persuade the Chinese authorities to do blood tests for NoFear in some of those cases."

Brogan paused so long Mac checked to be sure the connection was still live. It was, and Brogan said finally, "Have you thought of giving up neurosurgery? I could use an analyst who thinks like you."

Three weeks later, Brogan Zoomed Mac. "I'm calling about your insane prediction that NoFear would start to appear in China despite the government's blockade."

"And?" Mac asked.

"It's happening already. Our Shanghai operatives report increasing numbers of young people taking the supplement."

"How do you know they're taking NoFear?"

"Illegal market transactions, young people involved in crazy stunts, some blood work on people who have died in unusual ways. NoFear is showing regularly on postmortem blood tests in many deaths. There's a definite rise in all indicators."

"So, what's the plan?" Mac asked, ambivalent about the news. He had predicted NoFear infiltration from his experience with cancer cells, but he reminded himself that the tumor ultimately killed the host. Was he looking at the imminent destruction of society world-wide?

"Wait for the NoFear boomerang to return to the people that threw it into the air. Perhaps then we can get some international cooperation in eliminating the damned stuff."

不怕

CHAPTER THIRTY-TWO

MAC'S LUNCH WITH THE HARBOR HOSPITAL CEO

ALGO CLUB, BOSTON

Many people underestimated Susan Renwick, President and Chief Executive Officer of Harbor Hospital.

Mac was not one of them.

Renwick was petite, attractive, and smart. She understood that a hospital existed for patients. Her Ph.D. in social work might have been looked down on by M.D.s if she were a less capable leader, but she had guided the hospital through COVID and beyond with great wisdom. She was an administrator Mac respected.

When he received an invitation to lunch with her at the Algo Club in Boston's Back Bay, he accepted with a combination of curiosity and apprehension. Her administrative assistant would not say what it was about. Mac was still anxious about his surgery at Lincoln Hospital. Operating on a teenager had angered Harbor's Chief Medical Officer, and Mac wondered whether that anger had percolated to the Harbor Hospital CEO and Board of Trustees.

Elegant in a tailored suit, white shirt, and bow tie, he left his car with the valet attendants at the front of the building.

He had known the club as a tired townhouse filled with

ancient men but heard that it had been sold.As he entered the building, he realized that the new owners had carried out substantial renovations. The most important change appeared to be in the membership. In place of a stuffy gentleman's club he found a crowded building pulsing with energetic young men and women.

Dr. Renwick was waiting for him at the door, matching his sartorial elegance with a navy-blue Dior suit. They lunched in the informal bistro, cheerful and bright from its southern exposure on the Commonwealth Avenue mall. The reception area smelled of lilacs, and the aromas from the open kitchen mixed in garlic, basil, and marjoram.

"Thanks for driving into Back Bay to meet," Renwick began. "I thought you might like to see what imagination can do with an old Georgian building. Besides, it's a delight for me to get away from the hospital."

Mac looked around at his fellow diners, every color and gender, selecting from a menu that could be gluten-free, vegan, dairy-free, low-calorie, or traditional.

Mac chose broiled salmon and broccoli. Renwick ordered a Caesar salad.

Mac hoped his anxiety at what the meeting involved was not too obvious.

As if reading his mind, Renwick began, "I'm sure you're worried about my invitation to lunch at a fancy Boston club far away from the hospital." She smiled. "I just wanted to share good news in a setting with no other hospital personnel present." She extended her right hand. As a reflex, he shook it before he knew why he should.

"Doctor Duncan MacGregor," she said. "Today you are officially the first chief of the new department of neurosurgery at Harbor Hospital."

She laughed and paused while Mac let the news sink in. Relief flooded his body. He grinned with a shake of his head. He had worried for months that someone antagonistic to him and his ideals might be given the position, knowing the chair of the search committee was not a friend.

Renwick's smile broadened. "I'm sorry it's taken so long, but you know the process. We have to get buy-in from chiefs, from nursing and administrative staff, and from the University. That's all past history now. In spite of, or perhaps because of, your international work, we got universal support for you to take the job. I have to admit that an important element was Mr. Zadi's endowment of the department chair as long as you got the job. But the fact remains that you are the principal icon of our hospital, and I am proud to acknowledge that."

They ate their meal discussing the role of a chief, the importance of interaction with others, and the complexity of the present political and health care systems. When they had finished, Renwick stood and shook his hand. "Big congratulations to you, Mac. Please don't say anything to hospital people about this until the official announcement tomorrow. Of course, you can tell Lauren and the children. I'm really excited to work with you in the coming years."

不怕

CHAPTER THIRTY-THREE

THE WHITE HOUSE SPEAKS

BROOKLINE, MA

Mac announced his promotion at the dinner table that evening. Maggie clapped enthusiastically. "My Dad's going to be a chief! Wait 'til I tell the other girls at school."

"Please, not for a couple of days," Mac said. "I'll let you know when you can talk about it. For now, it has to be our secret."

"What does a chief do anyway?" Peter asked.

"He's like the principal at school," Mac said.

"I hope you're nicer than Mr. Clark," Peter said. "He's way strict."

"Your father will be a great chief," Lauren said. "I just hope he allocates appropriate time for his administrative duties and doesn't just add them onto a schedule that's already way too busy." She shot Mac a glance that carried the message only too clearly.

"What are administrative duties?" Peter asked.

"All the things a chief has to do," she replied, looking at Mac with a tilt of her head that he knew meant trouble. "But let's talk about you. You have two hours for homework, then bedtime," she said to the children, starting to clear the table as they sprinted off.

"What's wrong?" Mac asked as he helped her clean up. "Aren't you pleased?"

"Of course I'm pleased. Being chief is terrific, and I know you've been worried about some person you don't like taking the position. I just hope you plan to give up other activities, like maybe your political and international stuff."

Mac frowned. "I'll have to work that out. I really enjoy the chance to help global neurosurgery. I think it's an important part of being in the United States."

"Sure, like you've helped with that NoFear issue? You spent a lot of time for nothing on that problem, in my opinion. And remember that you can't add any more hours to your day," she said, kissing him on the cheek.

"I've already put the problem of NoFear into the wastebasket of 'things I can't control,'" he said. "Don't worry."

Two days later, his secretary Sheila buzzed him when he was in the laboratory. "I know you don't want to be disturbed, but this caller says she's from the White House."

"Name?"

"Janice Lake."

"Put her through."

"Mac? This is Janice Lake. I apologize that you might hear some beeps on the phone because this is a secure line."

"Are you calling about Lucy? Is she OK?" Mac asked.

"Better than OK. In the four months since her surgery, she's discarded her rebel approach to life, gets A's instead of C's, takes no medicines, and wants to be a neurosurgeon. I'm sure that's not a usual side effect of brain surgery, but Bruce and I are grateful every day for what you did."

"Please give her a hug for me. I'm delighted she's recovering well."

"I will. She'll be glad to know we talked. She's still chuffed about the incision, all hidden by hair, but there if she wants to show her best friends." Her tone changed. "But I'm calling about NoFear. You and I both know that's the drug that caused Lucy's injury. I told President Barker her story, and he says there are many similar accounts coming from every state. It's a dangerous supplement and should be banned."

"And the congressional committee report will deny all that?"

"Yes. Their report is a complete whitewash. The President is as angry as I am about the way the MARA people stonewalled any real investigation. He smells the same sort of influence he attacked when big pharma kept insulin prices so high. Key congressional players influenced by lobbyists are blocking the truth. That's not the American way."

"I think there might be influence from outside the United States as well," Mac said.

"That's the main reason for my call. The CIA director has evidence NoFear is being funded by the Chinese government to destabilize the United States. He wants to form an informal group to help decide the best option to move forward. We would like you to join that group."

"Will it have more likelihood of success than the congress committee?"

"Yes. And the CIA rep will be Jim Brogan, a man you know. Will you serve?"

"Yes. I'd be glad to help."

"That's terrific," Janice said. "It may take a month to set it up, but perhaps we can get some resolution to the NoFear problem by using international collaboration. It's a long shot, but we're running out of options, and the president wants to create a group effort rather than trying to go this alone."

不怕

PART THREE

NOFEAR INFILTRATES CHINA

不怕

CHAPTER THIRTY-FOUR

NOFEAR FLIES

SHANGHAI, CHINA

Heart pounding, nineteen-year-old Chu Jua stared down at the city of Shanghai spread below him in the emerging light of a Sunday dawn.

His view from Shanghai Tower's top floor dwarfed regular high-rise buildings. Boats on the Huangpu River appeared to be tiny toys. He heard only wind whistling past the large access gate he had just opened. Smog wrapped the tower as it did all Shanghai, and its acrid odor irritated his nostrils.

The machine room he had chosen as the jump site seemed perfect. Half the size of an airplane hangar, it contained only HVAC and elevator machinery. Its concrete floor led to an opening to the outside world ten meters wide and eight meters high, large enough to launch all the winged devices in the plan.

Access for Chu and his two friends had been simple once he had stolen the ID of a maintenance worker. They used the service elevators to take them to the 128th floor, not as fast as the tourist lifts, but still making Chu's ears pop with the speed of ascent. The elevators were capacious enough to hold the bags and paraphernalia of his flight team. As a bonus, one swipe of the purloined ID card opened the door to the mechanical room they now stood in.

Each team member would make history today, Chu thought with pride. They had a common goal—to prove their apparatus could fly safely from a six-hundred-meter height to a small city park. Bo Jaling, female hang-gliding superstar, would break the record for a city hang-glider descent. Zhan Ki, expert in parasailing, would do the same with his guided parachute. Chu himself would become immortal by demonstrating the possibility of human winged flight.

Months of dreaming, planning, and recruitment would climax in less than an hour. Chu would glide with synthetic wings from the tallest building in China to a quiet park on the other side of the Huangpu River. People said this can't be done, but NoFear told him otherwise. He would join Daedalus and Leonardo DaVinci in the history of human flight.

"Anyone want a top-up before we launch?" he asked, offering two NoFear capsules to each of his companions along with a shared bottle of water.

"I do," Bo Jaling said as she began to assemble her hang glider. "I'd be a nervous wreck without that pill."

"I take all the NoFear I can get." Zhan Ki said, swallowing his capsules without any water as he pulled the billowing nylon of his parasail out of a duffel bag.

"We'll go viral on Tik-Tok," Chu said, unfolding large nylon wings in preparation for strapping them to his arms. "Our friend Wan Ji waits on the observation tower of the Ping An Center to record our flights, and three classmates in other buildings will record our progress as we descend."

"We're definitely creating history," Zhan said, echoing the atmosphere of excitement that reverberated in the mechanical room. He turned to the others. "Let's have a contest," he shouted. "First person to get their equipment assembled gets to jump first."

"No fair," Bo said. "You only have to attach your seat harness to the parasail and you're done. Chu and I must assemble our entire machines."

"Too bad," Zhan replied as he dragged his bright red parasail across the floor to the garage-door-sized opening that led to the skies of Shanghai. He attached himself to the seat hanging under the parasail with a wink and a wave.

Bo looked up, inserting rigid rods to reinforce her three-meter triangular glider. She seemed to realize that she would not be first but shouted, "I call second." She clipped on the harness that would let her fly face down below the wings.

Chu wanted to go last so he could watch the others begin their flights and revel in the moment. Besides, by observing them he could assess the updraft pattern and anticipate any unexpected obstacles to the flight.

As he assembled his wings, he retraced in his mind the convoluted pathway to this monumental day. He had identified two like-minded students eager to fly, introduced them to NoFear so they would not back out, and practiced short flights in weekend trips to the western mountains. They were adventurers ready to take on a crazy project, and NoFear made everything possible.

He strapped on his revolutionary wings, with aerodynamic design meant to glide rather than flap and fly. That is where his predecessors in winged flight failed. Unlike them, he realized the human body does not have the musculature to flap wings fast enough to fly like a bird. Gliding is different. For that, it is only necessary to design the wings to create an uplift as they slice through the air. And that's what he had done, adding a few feathers to the structure for effect.

Chu watched with delight as Zhan threw his red parasail out of the opening into the haze. The wind caught it and tightened the ropes to the harness. Zhan was pulled into space by the suction of the passing wind and plummeted downward. Chu tensed at the thought his friend might smash into the tower. At the last minute, the parasail filled and yanked him away.

In the first few hundred meters of Zhan's descent, only a few supertall buildings interfered with a smooth pathway. Updrafts lifted him in a roller-coaster ride on the airways, but he navigated steadily toward the river that would provide a safe path to Binjiang Park.

Bo dove off the building next, showing her form as the experienced hang glider pilot she was. She dipped at first, then caught an updraft and sped above the launch pad. She flattened her course and reversed direction to swing back toward the tower. Chu saw her wave from her horizontal position under the glider as she expertly turned it and maneuvered toward the river.

Shouts and pounding on the door to the mechanical room suddenly interrupted Chu's surveillance of his friends. Massive machinery obstructed his view of the door, but he realized it was time for him to fly. Security guards must have been alerted to unusual activity early on this weekend day. He dragged his wings to the edge of the precipice and peered over the edge.

The Ping An International Finance Center appeared to his right and the Shanghai World Finance Center to the left beside the Oriental Pearl TV Tower.

Footsteps began to reverberate within the room and the shouting grew louder.

He dove, or rather was pulled out by the wind howling past the opening. He began to fall but captured an updraft to carry him away from the building.

All shouting faded as he floated above Shanghai. The tower he had just jumped from revealed its full audacity, a twisting of two shells around an inner core that made it one of the most beautiful buildings in the world as well as the third tallest.

Below him, dozens of modest high-rise towers dotted the landscape unlike any he had ever experienced during flight. The rush of wind filled his ears with a roar. The smoggy air irritated his eyes despite the goggles he wore. A light haze shrouded buildings even this distance above the street but did not interfere with the clarity of the images below. He felt elation he had never experienced, gliding like an eagle on the currents above a city of twenty million people.

Twenty million people who tomorrow would be talking about him and his companions.

The thought was insane!

He could see Zhan sailing far below, with the parasail now outlined against the Bund and the river. The vagaries of wind draft bounced the chute back and forth, but it steadily sailed toward the green patch of park they all wanted to land in. Chu lost track as it descended.

Halfway between him and Zhan, Chu could see Bo's glider weave past the Oriental Pearl TV tower toward the brown snaking river, like an aircraft heading for a landing strip. A passenger boat with a high smokestack swerved into the hang-glider's path and it lifted away, expertly avoiding the obstacle. The course correction meant Bo had to overshoot the park, catch an updraft and turn to land from the opposite direction planned. She carried out the maneuver smoothly and appeared to set down in a clearing without difficulty.

Chu saw the park clearly now and still had enough height to reach it.

The problem was the speed of his descent as he approached the park. The wind suddenly shifted, pushing him toward a clump of trees. One of his wings knocked a tree branch and shredded. He had no uplift now and fell like a rock. He barely had time to think, heart and head pounding as he worked to keep his feet downward so he would not break his neck in the landing.

The grass rushed toward him much too fast. He braced for impact and screamed as he hit the ground, legs fracturing and driving bone through muscle, skin, and clothing to expose shattered edges. Intolerable pain enveloped him.

不怕

CHAPTER THIRTY-FIVE

HAN INVESTIGATES

SHANGHAI, CHINA

Han Li's investigators spent several days researching the foolhardy attempt of Chu Jua and his fellow students to soar from Shanghai tower. A student named Zhan Ki had died, unable to navigate his parasail around Shanghai towers. Bo Jaling, the woman in the group, had suffered arm and collarbone fractures when she hang glided into the park. Chu himself, who appeared to be the ringleader, had been critically injured after a crazy attempt to use artificial wings to fly. Surgeons had spent ten hours putting his legs back together.

Han decided to investigate the situation himself to assess how much influence NoFear had on the episode. He was concerned that this compound had infiltrated China enough that the country was about to descend into chaos.

He sat at Chu's bedside in Shanghai's Changzheng Hospital, where Chu lay swathed in bandages. Both legs, encased in full-length casts, were suspended by pulleys.

The room was modern and clean, with continuous blood pressure, pulse, and oxygenation monitoring equipment and a bed that could assume multiple positions. A picture of Chairman Zhang hung on the wall.

The surgeons who had replaced Chu's shattered femurs with stainless steel rods had carried out world-class surgery. But why should a smart college student be in this predicament? Why did Chu think he could safely take winged flight from the tallest building in China? Why did his friend think he could parasail safely in the city before he smashed into the street and died? Why had normal common sense not stopped them from what amounted to a suicide mission?

Han thought of his own sixteen-year-old son and shuddered. As a member of the Politburo standing committee, he had the obligation to investigate Chu's insane flight attempt. If NoFear powered that flight, he needed to know.

"What made you think you could fly from Shanghai Tower?" Han asked, voice furious with disapproval.

Chu could barely summon enough energy to speak. "Seemed no problem but the trees…" He lifted his head off the pillow to stare at his plaster-cast legs and his bandaged arms and chest.

"Weren't you afraid?" Han asked.

"No."

"Why not?"

"NoFear," Chu said. "It removed all anxieties for me and my friends. We did take a lot more pills than we should have."

Han turned away. Had his attempts—or rather, Jin's attempts—to keep NoFear out of China failed?

"Where did you get NoFear?" he asked Chu.

"I don't remember exactly."

Han pounded a fist against Chu's bedside table. "Don't think you can hide your supplier's name from us. We'll track him down and—"

"No special dealers. Everyone sells NoFear," Chu said, dropping his head back onto the pillow.

Han paced for several seconds trying to collect his thoughts. "We could imprison you for the rest of your life," he finally said, "but I'll make a deal with you. If you publicly denounce NoFear and what it has done to you, we will allow you to go back to school when you have healed. We need persuasive young voices to stop the spread of this dangerous drug."

He waited, saw no response from Chu.

"Well, I am waiting," Han announced. "Nod yes or no."

Chu opened his eyes and nodded.

"I'm keeping a police guard at your door to stop anyone from approaching you. You may only speak when I am in the room. Do you understand? I want the distribution of this drug stopped."

不怕

CHAPTER THIRTY-SIX

NOFEAR LARPING

BEIJING, CHINA

Two days later, Han received a cell phone call that chilled him to the bone. “Dad, I’m scared. Can you come get me?”

He recognized his son’s voice despite the noisy background.

“Of course. Where are you, Cheng?” He tried to sound calm, looked at his watch—five p.m. *Why was his son not in school?*

“The China National Convention Center.”

“In Chaoyang? Why are you there, and what’s going on?” Han’s pulse raced. He didn’t like surprises, especially from his own family.

“After school a bunch of my classmates decided to go the Convention Center to watch the Beijing Major Dota 2 video game competition.”

“But...” Han sputtered.

“I know, I know. We were supposed to go to soccer practice. But the final gamer teams were competing for a three-million-yuan prize. Listen, can you just come get me?”

Han realized Cheng was crying. “Are you safe?” he asked.

"Sort of. It's just that something weird happened. I don't want to be here anymore. The subways and buses have been completely blocked. I can't get away."

Panic began to creep into Han's brain. *How do you find one boy in a convention center that holds thirty thousand people*? "Can you see the Grand Hotel?" he finally asked.

"Yes."

"Go to the concierge desk there and wait for me. Can you do that? Did you hear what I said?"

"Yes, father. I'll find it. Please hurry."

Han disconnected and called the Politburo personal deployment center, the center that arranged travel exclusively for the inner circle of the Politburo, the oligarchy that ruled the People's Republic of China. Han demanded to speak to the director. "I must get to the International Convention Center in Chaoyang right away," he said once he reached him.

"Hold a moment," the director said. Ten seconds later he returned. "You can't get close by car. There's a riot going on. A helicopter is the only possible way."

"Where would it land?"

"The North Star Continental Grand Hotel has a helipad on its roof. It was created for Olympic VIPs."

"Perfect. Get me a helicopter. Right now."

Zhongnanhai, the location of Han's office, had a helipad behind it. In ten minutes a Eurocopter AS 332 set down to transport him. He ducked under its rotors within moments of its arrival. "Convention Center at Fourth Ring," he barked at the pilot and belted himself in.

The vibration of the speeding bird shook his bones. The deafening sound of the rotors beggared conversation and thought. The smell of ozone permeated his nostrils, and the cabin was freezing.

As Han reached the convention center, his discomfort was replaced with anxiety.

He had trouble believing what he saw. Thousands of people filled the parking lot around the building and spilled into the fourth ring freeway which encircled Beijing.

He could not make out their outfits clearly, but they seemed to be superheroes and princesses and politicians and assassins, all dressed in brightly colored costumes. They stopped traffic for kilometers around the center, covering cars with foam, painting them with spray paint, occasionally smashing their windows. Drivers left their cars in the middle of the street and ran. Police in combat gear tried to contain the mob.

"Set us down in the hotel's heliport," Han shouted to the pilot. A few minutes later, he stepped onto the helipad and raced for the elevator to the ground floor.

Chaos reigned in the hotel reception area just as it had in the parking lot. Hundreds of people of all ages filled the space with demands to get to their rooms. They shouted complaints, wailed, and cursed.

So much for the idea of the restrained Chinese citizen, Han thought. Something was affecting these people in a way Han had never seen before. And the people in the hotel lobby were not all dressed in weird garb. Most of them appeared to be normal citizens.

Han pushed toward the concierge desk and sighed with relief when he saw his son Cheng cowering beside it.

"Are you OK?" he asked as they embraced. He realized this was an inappropriate public gesture but did not care.

"I'm OK, but I'm still really scared," Cheng answered.

"Follow me," Han said and began to navigate his way through the crowd.

After they had climbed into the Eurocopter, Han began his son's interrogation. "What made you decide to go to the gaming tournament?" he asked the terrified boy.

"A bunch of my friends suggested we forget our soccer match to go to the gamer finals at the convention center. I was afraid to turn them down," Cheng replied.

"Were those friends taking NoFear?" Han asked.

"Everybody is," Cheng said, "except me."

"What happened next?"

"We arrived and found seats to watch the final videogame teams play. A lot of people wore Cosplay costumes to identify with their favorite video characters. After half an hour, one of their leaders said something like 'This is boring. We need to LARP.'"

"What's LARP?" Han asked.

"Live Action Role Play," Cheng said. "It moves video games into real life. Most of the people in the audience ran through the exits into the parking lots and streets around the center. The place emptied. I had no choice but to follow."

"And was NoFear involved?" Han asked.

"Of course," his son replied. "It's my friends' new favorite pill."

"Where do they get it?"

"Everywhere."

"Have you taken it?"

"I already told you. No." Cheng looked directly at his father as if his stare would confirm he was telling the truth.

"Why didn't you take it?"

"I was afraid of what you would do to me. I pretended to swallow some with the others but spit it out."

Han believed his son. They travelled back to the office together while Han contemplated the implications of what he had seen in the last week. Fortunately, the helicopter was so noisy it allowed no conversations. Han knew by the time they returned that NoFear was now a problem within China.

不怕

CHAPTER THIRTY-SEVEN

THE POLITBURO SPEAKS

BEIJING, CHINA

As Han suspected, the Live Action Role Playing of three thousand gamers could not be covered up by the government, even with bots and social media disinformation. Television reporters from China and the West, social media leaders, and newspapers including Reuters, the Guardian, and the Times, dissected the event for days. The government shut down Tik-Tok to try to diminish the flood of videos and comments about the "brutal police suppression of a spontaneous and joyous LARP."

Only a few of the reports commented that most participants had used NoFear.

From interviews with his son and colleagues, Han became convinced that this dietary supplement was the primary cause of the riot. The participants he talked to, some arrested, some not, said they were taking NoFear regularly.

The compound he had sponsored as a weapon against the United States had boomeranged to disrupt his own country.

Han had an obligation to bring these findings to the other six members of the Politburo Standing Committee. This group, the innermost circle governing The People's Republic of China, shared responsibility for its 1.4 billion citizens. Han spent many days contemplating the best way to present his findings and opinions.

On the morning chosen to discuss the LARP episode, the committee gathered as usual in the small meeting room of Qin Zheng Hall in Zhongnanhai, the central government building next to Tiananmen Square. The seven men sat around a table in dark suits, white shirts, and dark ties, in a sparsely decorated room dominated by a huge portrait of Chairman Mao hanging on the wall. The Secretary-General of the Politburo, who also carried the title of President of the People's Republic of China, called the meeting to order.

The agenda began with the LARP disruption in Beijing, which Han felt was being given disproportionate weight by the council.

Zhao Xuexiang, ranking senior member, began the conversation. "Seeing the chaos during the videogame convention here in Beijing, we must cancel all future videogame competitions."

"That will not end the problem we face," Han said.

"Because?" Zhao asked.

"The problem is not the video games," Han replied. He took a long pause to consider his response as the other members stared at him. "The problem is NoFear."

"What does fear have to do with this?" Zhao asked. He had opposed Han in the past because of a belief that the traditional ways were the best approach to all problems. Han had the opposite belief, that China must move into the full complexity of the twenty-first century.

"Not fear," Han said. "A compound called NoFear. We have discussed it several times."

"The compound that was supposed to destroy America?"

Zhao asked with a sardonic tone. "I told you that strategy would not work when you proposed it months ago. Now we see the result of your poor judgment."

Han harbored a personal dislike for this man which he could not express openly. He knew that Zhao would capitalize on the failed NoFear plan and make animosity toward Han appear to be pure professional criticism. That would be devastating for Han's standing in the committee and Politburo as a whole.

Han sipped a glass of water. "Unfortunately," he said to his colleagues, "Comrade Jin failed in his mission to keep NoFear out of our country. My informants tell me that an underground market now distributes NoFear from manufacturing plants around the world, making it impossible to control the production. Some of those plants are ours, but Russia quietly built several and took over others we had created. NoFear is now a worldwide problem, with many unregistered facilities producing it. We only control a few of the facilities involved."

Kwan Jiguan, the Oxford educated youngest member of the council, interjected. "I understand why Russians might use this compound to attack us along with the United States. China could be destabilized as easily as America. That would leave Russia the strongest country still standing."

"Then we should make its use illegal in China," Zhao said. "We have an obligation to stop it."

"Making it illegal all at once would be a bad idea," Han said.

"What do you mean?" Zhao said, leaning forward in attack mode. "You just told us the compound is too dangerous to have on the streets. Now you say we shouldn't forbid it. Make up your mind."

"So many people use it," Han replied, "that a sudden ban could cause violent riots."

"Your opinion," Zhao said, "but do we have any real proof that NoFear use is as widespread as you claim? Perhaps a ban would have no ill effects." With a sly smile he added. "You may be too emotional about this, comrade. My friends tell me your son was involved in the Beijing demonstration." He wagged his index finger at Han as if accusing him of a crime.

The men turned toward Han.

"My son was there," Han said, "because he was afraid to say no to his friends."

"Doesn't sound like he was using NoFear," Kwan said, smiling as if to lessen the tension. "If you're right about its effects, he wouldn't be afraid of anything."

"Maybe it just didn't work for him," Zhao said, trying to recover the offensive. "What did he say about his friends' use?"

"He didn't know how much they used, but he did say everyone he knows has tried NoFear one time or another."

"Are you sure he's not taking the stuff?" Zhao asked.

"He says not. Fear of me and his mother keeps him from trying it."

The Secretary-General of the politburo spoke for the first time. "Comrades, I think we have debated this issue enough. Can we get a consensus? How many think we should ban NoFear immediately, making its sale and consumption illegal in our country?"

Four members put up their hands.

"How many favor another tactic?"

Han and Kwan raised theirs. The Secretary-General did not vote.

"It's unanimous," the Secretary-General said. "We will ban NoFear at once. Send out the appropriate notices and have police and the military begin the embargo. I did not vote formally but agree with prohibiting it. It is imperative that we stop this drug now."

不怕

CHAPTER THIRTY-EIGHT

APPROACHING TIANANMEN SQUARE

BEIJING, CHINA

From his vantage point in the Great Hall of the People, Han Li shuddered as he surveyed Tiananmen Square, the showplace of China.

Below him, thousands of Beijing citizens gathered to protest the NoFear ban the Politburo had just imposed. He had warned his colleagues about the consequences of their action. Why had they not realized the uprising the embargo would cause?

He had often watched military parades in this space, had been a teenager in 1989 when a student demonstration in Tiananmen Square led to brutal suppression by the government. The memory of that event, when some of his friends were killed, had been one of the driving factors in his decision to enter government service.

Smaller demonstrations had occurred throughout the country in the two weeks since the NoFear ban, but the protest he faced now promised to be a full-scale disaster. The people he saw in the plaza were not just students. They were citizens from every Chinese ethnicity and every age, men and women, and some with children.

They carried placards with slogans unimaginable four months ago.

Do not stop NoFear.

NoFear or Death

Stop the NoFear ban!

Mothers against NoFear

In 1989, no one would have protested a government edict with placards. Something today had made them fearless, and that something was NoFear.

Han turned with a look of alarm toward the other six committee members observing the demonstrators from the same viewing stand, protected by a thick transparent screen from any projectiles. They seemed as perturbed as he. The shouts of the crowd created a background of anxiety. Chinese citizens did not protest in this way.

On the ground, demonstrators climbed the Tienanmen Square Statue of Liberty, erected to commemorate the 1989 massacre of students. The agitators tried to topple the Monument to the People's Heroes, swarmed like ants over the Mausoleum of Mao Zedong, and tried to break into the shuttered National Museum of China. The police and military that normally patrolled the square were overwhelmed by a tsunami of fearless protestors.

This was not the China Han knew, and he was terrified. The old China had respectful and obedient citizens, willing to subjugate themselves to the needs of the whole country. This looked more like the United States—demonstrators going wild, loss of order, political chaos.

The members of the Politburo shook their heads. Zhao spoke first. "We cannot let this unrest continue. It is necessary to restore order in our most important public space."

Han challenged him. "How will you do that? These

people are lit up with a drug that makes them fearless. They will jump off buildings, attack soldiers with guns, and fight each other. There is no peaceful way to stop this protest."

The Secretary-General interrupted. "I do not believe this demonstration is good for the People's Republic. It must be stopped. I will authorize any means necessary to control and disperse the crowds. We will not vote on this measure. I have decided."

Han knew what this meant—a repeat of the 1989 massacre. He also understood why such a move was necessary. He was grateful that the Secretary-General had not asked for a consensus, in some way relieving the others present of responsibility.

Han looked at his watch. He had an appointment to see Jin on the ground outside the building in five minutes. He excused himself from his peers and moved through the throng to the meeting place he had selected.

不怕

CHAPTER THIRTY-NINE

TIANANMEN SQUARE REDUX

BEIJING, CHINA

Jin tried to take a deep breath. The oppressive pollution made extracting oxygen from the Beijing air impossible. The mob around him in Tiananmen Square shouted and jostled from every direction. The stench of sweat added to the feeling of suffocation. The chants of the protesting crowd drowned out all other sounds except the *rat-tat-tat* of occasional gunfire.

"Couldn't we watch this from the observation tower?" Jin shouted at Han, his boss, who had demanded this meeting.

"You must observe up close what you have caused," Han shouted, spreading his thick arms at the devastating scene spread before them.

All around him, Jin saw chaos, young men and women facing military personnel and equipment without clear fear. Chanting "TIME FOR CHANGE," they marched in clusters. If they met soldiers with rifles at the ready, they attacked. Some were shot as they advanced, but a significant number of the military put their weapons down and walked away from the advancing mob.

"Hundreds have died here today," Han shouted, "both soldiers and demonstrators."

"But why do you think I have anything to do with this demonstration?" Jin quaked at his boldness in challenging his boss, but he knew he faced severe punishment if he became a scapegoat for this chaos.

Han slammed his fat fist into his own fleshy palm. "We analyzed blood samples from combatants we have arrested. They show NoFear at great concentration. Your drug is doing to us what we wanted to do to the United States."

"But I had nothing to do with NoFear getting onto our streets," Jin said. He started to back away but was blocked by two beefy men he did not know.

"You were ordered to develop NoFear as a weapon against the United States. My specific instructions were to keep it out of China. You failed. Somehow it has infiltrated our system. Under its influence, our own youth attack Chinese soldiers and block our tanks. Some are killed, but their colleagues do not seem deterred."

"I kept all official channels closed," Jin protested, looking wildly around him for support. "This is the underground market at work. I cannot be held responsible."

Han pierced Jin with an accusatory stare. "No matter. Despite your incompetence, we have arrived at a solution. Unfortunately, this will be similar to 1989, but extreme measures are necessary to combat extreme threats." He looked toward the far end of the square, where forty tanks began to roll toward the mob. "These vehicles are driven by mercenaries who have no sympathy for the demonstrators. The rioters will have two choices—run, or die."

Jin watched the advancing military vehicles with increasing anxiety. Some students tried to climb into tank turrets and were shot at pointblank range. A few lay in rows in front of the tanks and were flattened. The sounds of their screaming and the disbelieving look in their eyes as they were killed, imprinted themselves unbearably on Jin's brain.

As the behemoth tanks rolled toward his position, the screams of victims and crunching of bones as bodies disappeared under their treads froze Jin's body and mind. Implacable death machines, the tanks moved in formation, destroying whatever got in their way. They towered above the humans in the square, their camouflage and huge treads grotesquely out of place in the heart of Beijing.

The phalanx of steel monsters thundered through the square in savage synchrony. The earth shook and conversation became impossible. "They're heading right for us," Jin shouted. His heart raced and he felt as if he would pass out. "We have to get out of here."

"Not *we*," Han said, moving back into the crowd and nodding at the two beefy men who had been standing behind Jin.

Jin watched the massive tanks roll toward him, felt the overpowering roar of their engines, smelled the exhaust fumes spewing from their innards.

He turned to run.

One of the strongmen blocked him while the other pulled out a revolver and blasted him in the thigh. Jin collapsed, writhing, blood pumping from the wound.

The men kicked him into the path of a tank.

He screamed for help, tried to sit up and drag himself out of the way. Excruciating pain in his left foot signaled he was too late. He watched the tank treads crush one foot, then the other. The bones of both legs cracked and splintered, jutting through the skin as he stared in a final panic. His pelvis turned to mush a split second before he saw his guts rupture with an explosion of blood, stool, and urine. He prayed to his ancestors as he died.

不怕

CHAPTER FORTY-ONE

REACTION

BROOKLINE, MA

Mac sat glued to a special television report on the recent events of Tiananmen Square. He and his family observed tanks move into position as multiple attempts to disperse the demonstrators failed.

"I don't think we should watch this program anymore," Mac said.

"But Dad," thirteen-year-old Maggie replied, "We need to know what's going on. China will either be our best friend or worst enemy when I'm your age."

"How about scootching up to your room to finish your homework?" Lauren said. "In the morning, Dad and I can tell you what happened."

"Sounds good to me," Peter said, "except for the homework part."

"Maggie, you coming?" Lauren asked.

"Do I have to, Mom? Can't I watch at least a minute or two?"

"That's up to your father."

"You can stay if you promise to go upstairs as soon as I tell you to," Mac said.

Maggie stared at the screen, frowned, then asked. "Why are these people demonstrating? What are they fighting for?"

"They think they're fighting for the right to take a pill."

"Why do they think they can attack soldiers and tanks and win? That just seems stupid."

Mac knew the answer to that question but did not want to discuss it. The confrontation between unarmed students and soldiers had all the signs of NoFear—dangerous consequences not thought out completely. Watching the tanks begin to roll, he turned off the television and told Maggie to go up to her homework. "I'm sorry, pumpkin, but it's time to go upstairs."

"I'm too old to be called pumpkin," Maggie said with her nose in the air as she flounced up the stairs.

Mac called Brogan, his CIA ally, as soon as the children had left the room.

"I assume you're calling about Tiananmen Square," Brogan said. "When I told you we thought NoFear was getting into China by illegal market channels, I had no idea how quickly it would spread. Beijing and Shanghai are the main centers at the moment, but the rest of Asia will follow. The potential destruction is horrific!"

"Can we stop it?" Mac asked.

"Only by collaborative efforts. My counterpart at the Chinese Ministry of State Security has tested many of the demonstrators for NoFear. He found high concentration of the drug. The Chinese government doesn't want this any more than we do."

"Pandora's Box," Mac said. "Demons released can't be recalled."

"What do you mean?" Brogan asked.

"NoFear was synthesized from an ancient Chinese herbal remedy for anxiety." Mac said. "The original herb caused so much nausea no one took it more than once. The modified pill we're dealing with is easy to take. Once this Pandora pill is let out of the box, it can't be put back in."

Mac spent breakfast the next morning trying to explain to his children why tanks would run over living teenagers.

不怕

CHAPTER FORTY-ONE

THE NOFEAR ADVISORY COMMITTEE

INTERNET

The White House advisory committee on NoFear finally set up a Zoom meeting, hosted by Janice Lake.

Janice began by asking its forty members to introduce themselves. Each began with name and position, then described why they wanted to remove NoFear from circulation. Mac was impressed by the breadth and depth of its members, who ranged from parents to legislators to lawyers and pharma officials.

The first speaker, an epidemiologist from Johns Hopkins with shoulder-length brown hair and wire-frame glasses, was assigned the job of describing the NoFear problem among young people in the United States. Her first graph showed a four hundred percent increase in teenage suicides after this supplement became available in health food stores.

"But do you know how many of those teens were actually using NoFear?" a legislative participant interrupted.

"Hard to get those numbers," the speaker said, "but we believe that seventy percent of American children between thirteen and nineteen take NoFear at some time."

A second epidemiologist extended data to older age groups. He began with a graph showing that in the United States, domestic violence had increased five hundred percent in the last six months. Assaults were up two hundred percent. Suicides had escalated by one thousand percent. Road rage accidents were so common that many jurisdictions had stopped recording them.

The speaker showed a video of citizens descending on a judge's office with baseball bats to protest a decision supporting women's reproductive rights. Their demonstration turned violent when several protesters broke through the police line and smashed the office door open, then began to beat desks and anyone in batting range until the police could muster forces enough to stop them. "This kind of violence is now commonplace around America," he said. "The courts are overwhelmed with cases."

He turned to data from states that allowed easy access to guns. Graph after graph showed that murders, robberies, sexual assaults, and home invasions had quadrupled since NoFear had appeared on their shelves. Texas, Florida, Alabama had an average of three school killings a month.

"I think we've seen enough to describe the problem," Janice said after thirty minutes of devastating data. "Let's talk next about the mechanism of NoFear action."

Grace Wu led this section. She began by describing the *Bupa* plant and identification and synthesis of its active component to produce NoFear, then showed how the compound turns off fear mechanisms. She displayed the pathways mediating anxiety that weave through every part of the brain. Mac began to pace as he watched. Although he knew these pathways, Dr. Wu's three-dimensional multicolored images left him terrified about the power of this compound to deactivate a warning system ingrained in humans for evolutionary survival.

Wu then displayed how NoFear affects the locus coeruleus, suggesting the compound is highly addictive. As she closed, she emphasized how important fear is for safety. "Taking NoFear inactivates warning systems humans have relied on for thousands of years."

Jim Brogan introduced the "Challenges" section of the meeting. "My job is to tell you what we are dealing with in trying to stop NoFear production. Let's begin with three key players."

He flashed a blurry rotund Asian face on the screen "This is the best picture we have of Han Li, a senior member of the Chinese Communist Politburo. We believe he heads a Chinese initiative to disrupt American social and political life using NoFear as a bioweapon. The situation has changed in the last few months. Because NoFear is beginning to boomerang back into China, officials there are willing to discuss collaborative efforts to control it."

He flashed another face on the screen. "This is Jin, a Chinese government official responsible for NoFear marketing in the United States. His mission was to spread the re-engineered version of NoFear in America but keep it out of China. He has failed. There are increasing signs that social disruption is beginning in China just as it has developed here after NoFear was introduced to the health food market. Jin has not been seen in the last few weeks."

"I thought the drug was Chinese to start with. Why wouldn't they already have controls?" a young man with red hair interjected.

"It did originate from a Chinese plant," Brogan said, "but the NoFear we know has isolated the active part of the plant and synthesized it in a pill. An American neuroscientist named Sophie Grainger did this work."

Brogan finished by displaying a Caucasian face soft, chubby, rounded. "This man may be familiar to some of you. He is Sterling Underwood, an American lobbyist funded by both China and Russia. He has been responsible for introducing NoFear to hundreds of Americans, including Justice Tilson who killed a reporter and himself. Using the tropes of freedom to choose and immunity of dietary supplements from FDA control, he has been incredibly successful at blocking all attempts to regulate this compound."

After a long discussion, the parents, neuroscientists, policy advisers, lawyers, pharmacologists, and legislators in the meeting agreed on a goal to ban NoFear worldwide. They also agreed that achieving that goal would be difficult because of differing national interests and an apparent campaign in favor of NoFear in the United States.

"So what do we do?" a parent asked.

"Could we convince the manufacturers to stop production by showing how dangerous the drug is?" an ethicist asked.

"No," a strategic analyst replied. "Natural Supplements Inc. makes millions of dollars from NoFear sales. There's no way they would voluntarily withdraw the drug. And even if the drug lost money in production and sales, the Chinese government would back it up with a subsidy. I expect there's no possibility of voluntary withdrawal."

"Could we blow up the production plants?" a parent asked. "That would solve the problem."

"No," Mac answered. "I witnessed an attempt to do that in Istanbul. Production recovered quickly. There are many sites in different countries now manufacturing this compound. Knock out one, and two others will take its place."

"Why can't the FBI and CIA just arrest everyone associated with NoFear manufacture?" another parent asked.

Brogan answered. "First, NoFear is classified as a food supplement. It's perfectly legal for anyone to take it. From the reception Dr. MacGregor and Dr. Wu had at the FDA, I don't think we're going to get any regulatory agency to limit it. Second, in America, we don't arrest people for producing compounds like NoFear unless government agencies declare its manufacture illegal. That isn't likely to happen because of the roadblocks backed by lobbyists and paid-off congress members."

Mac raised his hand. "Could we use social media to deliver the message that NoFear is a dangerous compound? Get mega-influencers to issue a consensus statement against further NoFear manufacture?"

"How would that work exactly?" Janice Lake asked.

"Get President Barker to speak against the compound and the system that is protecting it. Would that be possible, Janice?"

"Maybe," Janice said. "I wonder if we could ask President Zhang of China as well." She paused and looked away from the screen. "Consider the impact of a joint statement against NoFear by the two most powerful leaders in the world. At this time in America, media shape policy. A joint Chinese and American statement against NoFear would be a major blow to the manufacturers and users of the drug."

"Exactly," Mac said. "If the two presidents made a plea at the United Nations to control or prohibit NoFear, their comments might be translated into political power. They could lead the World Health Organization to call for a worldwide NoFear embargo."

"A crazy idea," Janice said, "but it just might work! Certainly better than trying to get Congress to act. Maybe we could use the news and social media to accomplish something remarkable."

不怕

CHAPTER FORTY-TWO

TOWARDS A SOLUTION

WASHINGTON, D.C.

"What did your NoFear advisory group decide?" President Charles Barker asked Janice Lake the morning after the advisory committee met. He sat on a wing chair in front of the fireplace, Janice on the couch facing him.

She glanced at the paired portraits of Abraham Lincoln/ George Washington and Thomas Jefferson/Alexander Hamilton flanking the large portrait of FDR above the fireplace. They represented people of different beliefs working together for the greater good, a possible model for NoFear regulation.

"Everyone agreed NoFear must be controlled," she began.

"Anyone with half a brain knows that," POTUS said. "The Congressional committee report was a bunch of malarky. They used the same old trope that freedom to choose must be honored as they did in allowing assault weapons, claiming freedom should allow people to kill anyone they hate."

He looked past the Resolute Desk through the bay window to the garden. "I don't understand the huge resistance to limiting this infernal drug. I've even been warned the Supreme Court would overturn an Executive Order to ban NoFear."

He turned toward Janice again. "Let's get to the point. What did the advisory group suggest we do to stop this damned drug?"

"You're not going to like their recommendation."

"Try me."

"They think you and President Zhang of China should make a joint statement against NoFear to the United Nations, setting the stage for a World Health Organization and Interpol ban. They didn't believe individual national governments would take the necessary steps to ban the substance because of Chinese and Russian interference."

"They're right about the Russians and Chinese working to keep the stuff available, but how did they get the idea that a joint effort to ban it might work? First, there's no chance Zhang would agree. China designed this drug as an attack on us. Zhang's not going to try to stop it," Barker said with a note of irritation. "Second, the UN has no power to restrict anything."

"Not so sure about Zhang, sir. Jim Brogan, the CIA director for terrorism, is on the committee. He says China's plan to create chaos in the United States using NoFear has backfired. The drug is flooding China through the underground economy and the government can't stop it. You saw the disaster in Tiananmen Square. Failure to limit NoFear penetration back into China shows the inadequacy of restrictive policies in today's world."

"Which might make a joint meeting more reasonable?"

"The committee thinks so. People thought NATO had no power when you revived it to confront the Russian invasion of Ukraine. The same could happen for NoFear. Maybe the United Nations could emerge as a practical force for good."

"Maybe," Barker said. "I need to get some more data. We can put it on as our first item on tomorrow's schedule."

The next morning's meeting was less contentious. "I verified everything you said about the infiltration of NoFear into China," President Barker said. "Asked the State Department to explore the possibility of an official visit from President Zhang. They did. In two hours, they reported the answer was 'No'. Said it was 'not a propitious time'."

"They probably think meeting with us will make the Russians mad," Janice said.

"Whatever. Anyway, it was a worthwhile idea, better than I thought when I first heard it. I like the idea of trying to strengthen the UN as the body to begin this kind of international medical collaboration. Lord knows, we need it if we ever have anything like COVID-19 again."

"Can we keep trying? I think it's our only chance."

"I don't want a lot of negotiation about a possible meeting. There would be too much pushback if the news got out to the press."

"May I ask an impertinent question, Sir?"

"That might already be one," Barker said with a smile. "Go ahead."

"Would you allow me to talk directly to my counterpart in Beijing?"

"No. I know you speak fluent Mandarin, but it would not be beneficial for you to get involved with negotiation in China. Women have no voice in Chinese national government. No Politburo members are female, and only 5% of significant government leadership positions are held by women. Anything you said would be discounted at once."

"With due respect, Sir. I don't want teens around the world dying from this drug."

"The answer is still No."

"Mr. President, whenever I think about my daughter Lucy and the injuries she sustained after taking NoFear, I realize she could easily be dead. I was just fortunate that Dr. MacGregor was there. Other parents around the world may not be as lucky."

The president's tone softened. "How is Lucy, Janice? I know it must be hard for you to be down here when she's in Massachusetts healing from her injuries."

Janice smiled, aware again of the empathy that had drawn her to accept President Barker's offer to be chief of staff despite the family sacrifices she knew it would require. "She's in full-time school and seems a lot less rebellious than she used to be."

"Bless her. She always reminds me of you. Tell her I send a big hello."

"I will, and she will be excited to know you asked about her. Every time I talk to her, I think of all the vulnerable young kids around the world and how lucky she is to be alive. I hate the idea of NoFear being freely available to anyone, American or Chinese."

"OK," Barker said. "I'll make a deal. If you have a State Department official on the line when you make the call and stop if they ask you to, you can try. Just make the connection fast and quietly so rumors don't start to spread. I don't want the New York Times saying we're begging President Zhang to come to the United States."

"I'll make the call at nine tonight with a senior State Department official on the line. I promise to stop the minute he asks me to."

Later that day Janice discovered that President Zhang had just named Kwan Jiguang, the chief of ideology and number five leader of the Communist Party, as his new chief of staff. This was the logical person for her to talk to.

She called Nick Rivers, the China Coordinator and Deputy Assistant Secretary of State for China and Taiwan at the State Department, to ask whether he could listen to her call.

"Say again?" Rivers asked.

"The President asked me to talk with Zhang's chief of staff about a meeting in the United States, but wanted to be sure State was represented. I'm planning to call at nine tonight and would like you to join me. We can do it remotely if you have a secure phone."

"Of course I have a secure phone," Rivers said, "but why are you trying to do this? My office has already explored the idea. The Chinese answer was a resounding NO."

"POTUS would like to try one more time. He really wants to make this work. Can you join me tonight?"

Rivers reluctantly agreed.

Janice initiated the call from her White House office so a tracker would legitimize its origin. She met with layers of telephone blockade before she got to the Chinese President's new chief of staff. She could imagine Rivers smirking as he listened.

"Chief of Staff Kwan Jiguan?" she asked in her perfect Beijing Mandarin.

"Yes. Who is this?"

"Janice Lake, the Chief of Staff for the President of the United States. I want to congratulate you on your new position with President Zhang. I am calling to ask you to arrange a meeting between our bosses."

"This is not the way. You must go through channels."

"I understand. I'm calling on a more personal level. Kwan Jiguang, do you have children?"

He paused, then answered with pride in his voice. "I have two children, thanks to the beneficence of the Chinese Communist Party in relaxing the restriction on children."

"Then you might understand why I am calling. It's about a drug called NoFear that originated with the *Bupa* plant."

"Yes, I am familiar with this drug."

"My teenage daughter almost died when she jumped from a stair landing after taking it. Can you imagine such a thing happening to one of your children? Our consultants have predicted that NoFear will soon be appearing in China. They suggested that the only way to get NoFear under control would be to have President Zhang and President Barker give a joint address to the United Nations about its dangers."

"That is impossible."

"I ask you, parent to parent, to think about your children. They are more important than political positions."

There was a pause on the line. Janice could hear Kwan Jiguan breathing hard.

"Esteemed Kwan Jiguan," Janice spoke again, "Please consider my request. Thank you."

After Kwan hung up, Janice spoke to State official Rivers, who was still on the line. "Any problems with what I said?"

"No, except it won't work."

Two days later, President Barker notified Janice that President Zhang had made a formal request to the State Department. Zhang's letter noted that, concerned about the infiltration of the American drug NoFear into China, he proposed that President Barker join him in a joint address to the United Nations. Together they might stop or limit the worldwide distribution of this so-called dietary supplement.

POTUS shook his head. "I don't know how you did it, Janice, but thank you. Now let's see what happens when two so-called rivals agree on something."

不怕

PART FOUR

TAMING THE TIGER

不怕

CHAPTER FORTY-THREE

UNDERWOOD GETS NEW ORDERS

GEORGETOWN, D.C.

Relaxing in his Georgetown townhouse with a snifter of brandy, Sterling Underwood answered a ring tone unique to one caller.

"*De La Cruz Art Gallery,* seven a.m. tomorrow," the speaker said, then disconnected without identifying himself.

Underwood cursed. The call was from Viktor Karpov, Underwood's Russian contact. A prominent oligarch in New York, Karpov claimed he had renounced his connections with Moscow's present political leadership. Underwood doubted that and despised Karpov's coarse manners. He did not despise the monthly stipend Karpov provided.

The call made Underwood worry that something was about to shift, probably for the worse. An in-person meeting was not their usual business arrangement.

Underwood resisted the urge to hurl his cell phone at the wall. He knew the De La Cruz Art Gallery. It fronted on Prospect Street not far from the previous site of the infamous statue of Optimus Prime and the Exorcist steps. Why had his Russian boss ordered him to appear on short notice so early in the morning?

He could use Lama, his black and white Shih Tzu, as the

excuse for an early morning walk if he met anyone he knew. He named the insanely cute Tibetan dog after the Dalai Lama, the most important Tibetan contribution to the West besides Mount Everest. He loved to walk through Georgetown streets with her. The dog's black face, mustache, and floppy ears attracted other men in droves.

Not likely at seven a.m., though. And considering who he was meeting, that was fine.

Underwood didn't sleep well the night before the meeting. He got up at six, planning to leave his house early to get the encounter over quicker. Nuzzling Lama as he fastened the plaid harness over the dog's upper torso, he said in a baby voice, "Wake up, little Lammy. We're going for an early walk."

The dog barked once to signal his approval. Over the years, Underwood had come to understand that Lama was probably the only thing he really loved.

They walked, dog prancing ahead, marking every other tree for herself, as the early light of dawn began to illuminate the sidewalks. The air smelled fresh and only an occasional taxi driver interrupted the silence.

Underwood had no problem identifying Karpov as they rounded the junction of Thirty-Sixth Street and Prospect. Dressed in a black wool coat with fur trim, the Russian stood staring at the gallery window as if he were examining a Michelangelo sculpture. Karpov's bulky size, thick neck, and furtive eye movements made him look like a Russian spy.

Which he was.

The two men stepped back as though they were both trying to get perspective on the art work in the window. No one else was in the vicinity.

"We walk," Karpov said, and struck out along Prospect St. "United Nations meeting you must attend in two weeks."

"I've heard about it, a multinational attempt to block NoFear and destroy its manufacturing sites. I don't think I can get in. At least, I haven't been invited."

"We make sure you get invitation," Karpov said. "You must attend and also speak. Lives may depend on it."

"Whose lives?"

"Yours. Meeting today signals the start of a new relationship between us."

"What do you mean?" Underwood asked, instinctively scooping Lama up.

They approached the house used to film *The Exorcist*, a movie that still terrified Underwood. The most upsetting scene used the steep stairs beside the house they were about to pass, a staircase that Father Damien Karras tumbled down and died on in the movie's final moments. Seventy-five steps led from Prospect Street to Canal Street far below. Underwood's fear of heights gripped him as he looked down the steep incline.

"So far your role has been to persuade friends to take NoFear," Karpov said, stopping at the top of the stairs. "Now we change rules of engagement. You became active agent for us."

Underwood stopped too. "What are you talking about? I'm no Russian agent. I'm an American lobbyist. That's all I know how to do." He turned and started to walk away.

"We ask Lama to help explain." Karpov grabbed the dog.

"What're you doing?" Underwood shouted, looking around for someone to come to help. The street was empty.

Karpov dangled the dog by its harness over the seventy-five steps that descended almost vertically to the street below. The Shih Tzu twisted and flailed, barking pitifully.

Underwood ran toward Karpov but had to stop at the top of the stairway. Nausea and vertigo overcame him as he looked over the brink of the flight of steps. He stretched his arm toward Karpov. “Please don’t,” he pleaded as the Russian dangled the dog over the precipice. “What exactly do you want?” He began to pant and felt his heart rate accelerating with tunnel vision overcoming his sight.

“That’s better,” Karpov said as he drew the animal back from the abyss. “Remember what happens to dog can happen to owner. I call you soon, and you come to New York ready to go to UN.”

不怕

CHAPTER FORTY-FOUR

THE RUSSIAN PLAN

MANHATTAN, N.Y.

Karpov ordered Underwood to meet him in the lobby of New York's Plaza Hotel two days before the UN meeting on NoFear. Underwood complied because he adored the money Russia deposited in his offshore accounts. He also did not want to be thrown from a high hotel window like some other Russian collaborators he had known.

"I'm impressed," Underwood said after the door attendant welcomed them to the Palm Court. "Only the rich or famous get to enter here."

Karpov grunted and led him to a reserved window table.

My kind of people. Vuitton bags, Chanel suits, Gucci shoes, he thought as he made his way through the crowded tables.

"They put tables too close," Karpov said, scanning the room.

"What do you have to tell me?" Underwood asked, trying to take control of the conversation. "And why the United Nations? Its security is very tight—"

"We leave," Karpov said.

"But this is *the* place to be seen in New York."

"Exactly. Not good."

Karpov navigated back to the exit. Underwood trailed after him, feeling like a dog following its master. The door attendant raised an eyebrow but said nothing. *Karpov is a boor. Most people feel privileged even to get into the hotel lobby,* Underwood thought as they exited.

On Plaza Square, the smell of expensive perfume spiked the air. Nathan's hot dog and Halal shawarma food carts sported lines of customers. Pedestrians filled the sidewalks and streamed to the Apple store across the street. The afternoon sun warmed the air into the eighties.

"We go into the Park," Karpov said. "I need exercise."

Was Karpov's grimace an attempted smile?

They entered the broad walkway into Central Park and passed the caricature and portrait artists hawking their work. Karpov pointed to a bench protected from the stream of visitors, horse-drawn carriages, runners, and cyclists.

"To answer your question," Karpov said after they sat, but without looking at Underwood, "your job is not to ask why anything. You follow orders."

"But I'm not one of your—"

Karpov put his hand up. "Face facts. We paid you well for NoFear promotion and distribution. Now want you do a much bigger job for us."

"What job?"

Karpov looked at the sky. "The Soviet Union was founding member of UN."

"Of course. Along with the Republic of China, France, the United Kingdom, and United States. They're the permanent members of the United Nations Security Council still."

"And all have veto power."

"So, the Russian Federation can block any resolutions it doesn't like," Underwood said. "Which it has done quite often, especially since the Ukraine invasion." He knew this was treacherous ground.

"Not invasion. Liberation. Anyway, some crazy people say Ukraine should have Security Council seat instead of Russia."

"But how—"

"UN Constitution gave seat to Soviet Union, which does not exist anymore. People say Ukraine could be considered successor to Soviet Union as much as Russia."

"That's crazy."

Karpov slammed his meaty fist into his hand. "Of course. On that we agree. But UN is still problem for us."

"You want to attack the UN? I'm sorry, but I'm not following."

"My boss wants me to lead attack on UN reputation. Important project. Keep NoFear weakening the degenerate Unites States. And weakening China too. I got job to make sure this continues and UN does not interfere." He wiped his brow. "I must do perfectly. Do not want to drop dead like other oligarchs."

"So what do you propose exactly?"

A homeless man wandered into their area. Karpov stood up from the bench and moved away from him back onto the sidewalk. Underwood followed.

"Better to keep walking," Karpov said. "We already discussed. You will be official speaker in General Assembly to argue for keeping NoFear, so you have easy access to hall and can sit in area reserved for speakers. We have arranged for you to be last person to speak before presidents. You will use skin-absorbed toxin we have employed since death of famous assassin Rhee Sung from DPRK. You put on gloves, load toxin on it, smear podium, and leave. Don't touch podium with bare hands."

"The whole podium becomes the assassin?"

"Yes."

"You mean you're asking me to murder the two most powerful leaders in the world?" Underwood's mouth dried. His vision clouded as a knot formed in his neck and a monster headache began.

"Just put some stuff on podium," Karpov said. "No guns, no knives."

"Won't they know it is me after the presidents collapse? How do I get away?"

"Melt into crowd. Throw gloves in some garbage bin," Karpov said. He stood and looked down at his lackey, who was still quivering.

"Now walk more alone and think about details," Karpov said. "Not good for us to be seen together. No—what you say—*interaction*— between us at UN. You understand?"

Karpov turned back toward Central Park South.

Underwood continued in the direction of the Metropolitan Museum. He wished his Shih-Tzu were there for discussion. The animal was his only confidant. His headache worsened by the moment, and there was no pain medication in sight.

Karpov's plan had too many uncertainties. Wouldn't the FBI or Interpol or whoever covered the UN test the podium? They would at once identify him as the assassin.

Karpov and his allies were setting him up.

He sat by the pool known as Conservatory Water, took a few extra NoFear pills, and considered what he might do. For the first time in his life, he felt trapped.

不怕

CHAPTER FORTY-FIVE

MAC IS INVITED TO THE UN

BROOKLINE, MA

Every evening, Mac tried to have dinner with his family. The table banter and discussion acted as an antidote to the desperate problems he had to deal with each day as a brain tumor surgeon. Around the family table he was just a dad.

This evening meal was chicken tikka masala and saag paneer delivered from a local Indian restaurant. After the food was demolished and a cascade of comments about school, friends, and other events finished, Mac said. "Jim Brogan asked me to go to the United Nations for a special session in three days."

"What's it about?" Maggie asked.

"A medication called NoFear," Mac said, noting that Lauren gave him a sideways glance. They had discussed his wish to control this compound many times.

"That's fire," eleven-year-old Peter said. "Can I go too? I'd be quiet."

"Sorry, can't happen. It's by invitation only," Mac said. "Security will be strict."

"Can you bring us back something from the UN? Not just a New York T shirt?" Maggie asked.

"I'll do my best to find something that meets your requirements," Mac said with a grin.

"At least it's New York, not Istanbul," Lauren said, with a look that reminded Mac he had been pretty much unavailable in his last days in Turkey. "I could drive down to get you if I had to."

"I'll do my best to stay out of trouble," Mac replied with a smile. "I'll be taken by limousine from one place to another. Besides, I don't have to go far away to find trouble."

He thought back to his experiences with a renegade North Korean assassin and a berserk paramilitary woman named Jane that had faced him right here in Boston within the last two years.

"Not funny," Lauren said. "Where will you stay?"

"The Millennium Hilton. It's just across the street from the UN."

"I'm not worried about you, Dad," thirteen-year-old Maggie said. "New York doesn't have a lot of violent crime. My civics teacher said lots of other cities are worse."

"New York doesn't even make the top ten list of violent cities in America," Lauren said. "How are you going to go, and when?"

"I'll take the Acela on Wednesday. The session is Thursday, and I should be back Friday. I wouldn't think anything bad is likely to happen in that short time."

不怕

CHAPTER FORTY-SIX

MAC ARRIVES AT THE UN

MANHATTAN, NY

The first recognition that his UN session might be problematic hit Mac as he arrived in New York on the fast train from Boston. Like other Acela passengers, he exited at the Moynihan Train Hall, a high-ceilinged space across Eighth Avenue from Pennsylvania Station. Enjoying this spectacular arrival hall was one reason he preferred to travel to Manhattan by train rather than plane.

Today, as he entered the hall, several hundred protestors carrying preprinted placards screamed epithets against the upcoming UN meeting to control NoFear. They chanted slogans loud enough to interfere with train announcements.

Mothers for NoFear!

NoFear forever!

Ban abortions, not NoFear!

Don't stand between us and our NoFear!

The pungent scent of marijuana drifted in the air. Dozens of New York police officers in riot gear reinforced the barriers surrounding the demonstrators, making the train hall look more like a military enclosure than a welcome center.

Mac could easily circumnavigate the protesters, but he worried about traffic toward the East River and the United Nations. Normally it would take less than half an hour to get across Manhattan to the Millennium Hotel at One UN Plaza. He had allowed himself two hours. He now realized that might not be enough.

Hustling through the hall, he exited to find his limousine among the cluster of chauffeurs and taxis at the corner of 8th Avenue and 33rd Street. In a city of eight million, he needed to identify the one person designated to transport him.

It turned out to be easy. One driver held an iPad with *Dr. Duncan* displayed on it. Mac climbed in grateful he didn't have to wait for his ride. He was used to having people consider his first name his last.

Maneuvering through the streets of New York always presented a challenge. Double-parked delivery trucks, one-way traffic systems, pedestrians stepping into the middle of the street, bicyclists cutting through the traffic...all typical impediments to crossing the island of Manhattan.

Today, however, he began to worry as obstacle followed obstacle. The distance from Penn Station to the Millennium Hotel was about two miles. After ninety minutes Mac had gotten to 44th Street and 2nd Avenue, half a block away from the hotel.

"What's with the traffic?" he asked the driver.

"Protestors around the UN," she answered. "And I can't take you to your hotel. 44th Street is one-way, and I couldn't get back out because of the crowds."

"I'll walk," Mac said, and stepped out with his small suitcase.

Hundreds of people filled 44th Street between him and the hotel. The New York Police Department had set up barriers to control the crowd. Waving banners and shouting "Leave us our NoFear," the demonstrators had changed the street into a pedestrian mall.

The police stopped him, checked his ID and hotel reservation. At the hotel entrance, a burly door attendant checked his name against a list, inspected his ID again, and gestured him into the lobby. The anxious woman at check-in said his room was not ready. She explained that they had experienced significant trouble getting staff to the hotel because of protestors, adding that she was worried about getting home herself. "It's like a war zone," she said.

Mac left his suitcase and exited to walk to the UN building two blocks away.

A phalanx of protestors faced him before he got halfway to the UN Plaza. One slight woman stepped directly into his path. "Going to the UN? You one of the people trying to take our NoFear away?"

Mac stopped, speechless. No way this woman could physically prevent him from moving past. Why would she think she could keep him from walking down a public street?

He knew the answer, of course. *NoFear.* Under its influence, she would step in front of a tank.

In seconds, a dozen other demonstrators surrounded the slight woman. A couple of them who looked more like soccer hooligans than protesters **could** block Mac. He wondered if they had been hired to encourage the disturbances and bring a touch of violence to them.

"Is this guy giving you trouble?" a hefty man Mac thought of as Bruiser asked.

"He's going to the NoFear meeting, I'm sure of that," the petite woman said. "Look at him with his white shirt and bow tie. Probably some kind of big shot."

"*Are* you going to the UN?" Bruiser challenged, taking several steps toward Mac and turning to the men advancing behind him. "Let's show this guy what we think of people trying to take NoFear from our wives and children."

A dozen demonstrators crowded toward Mac. He backed away, then turned and retreated to the hotel lobby, panting by the time he arrived. Bruiser and his friends followed him, but the beefy door attendant and police stopped them at the hotel entrance.

Shaken and breathing fast, Mac considered how unexpected the scene was and how dangerous the mob seemed. He called Brogan. "I'm at the hotel, but I can't get through the demonstrators to the meeting. A lot of them seem high on NoFear."

"It gets worse in the UN Plaza," Brogan said. "TikTok and other social media have been buzzing all day, telling people to protest. Videos encouraging violence have been taken down as quickly as they appeared, but the censors can't keep up with the volume."

"What should I do?"

"Stay right there. You're going to be strangely delighted."

不怕

CHAPTER FORTY-SEVEN

MAC'S TEAM ASSEMBLES

UN BUILDING, MANHATTAN

Mac waited in the lobby of the Millennium Hotel, admiring the lavishly decorated library and pictures of the hotel suites overlooking the East River. The Millennium UN Plaza hosted international dignitaries from every country.

Try as he might, he could not find anything "strangely delightful" about the scene until a familiar voice hailed him from a doorway behind him. "Doctor Mac?"

It sounded like Amara Zadi, the Moroccan police officer who had helped him recover from a blast injury last year. But that could not be. Amara was stationed in Lyon with the Interpol terrorist section.

He whirled around.

And recognized Amara at once. In an official Interpol uniform, she radiated the same joy that Mac felt. He laughed with delight.

"Bonjour, Dr. Mac," she said, moving toward him.

"Amara, it is you! How wonderful!" They embraced. "I thought it was your voice, but you're supposed to be in Lyon. What are you doing here in New York?"

"We in Interpol have been following the penetration of NoFear into the USA and the chaos that seems to follow it. We're worried about what will happen if it spreads to Europe and the rest of the world, which is certain to happen with our global economy. We want to create a database to help local authorities control it if the United Nations passes a resolution against it today. Brogan requested that I attend the meeting as a representative for the Interpol anti-terrorism division. He asked me keep my presence a secret to surprise you when we reconnected in the general assembly hall, but now I can help you get there!"

Mac stood back, filled with gratitude at seeing Amara well and happy. She appeared to have no scars from her harrowing ordeal on a container ship last summer "You look fabulous," he said. "How are your parents? And how did you get to the hotel through the mob so fast?"

"My family is fine. I'll tell you everything about them later. As for getting to the UN building, there's a secret passage from the hotel to the assembly hall. We should get going. Brogan wants to talk with you before the session."

She disappeared down a stairway to the basement, leading Mac to a door marked "No Entry." After unlocking it, she beckoned him to follow.

A tunnel stretched before them, well-lit and dry. It branched several times. Amara did not hesitate in choosing a path until she came to a closed door. Again, she turned a key and entered a tunnel darker and wetter than the first, perhaps used for steam pipes and electrical lines. It took several seconds for Mac's eyes to adjust to the semi-darkness. Amara kept walking at a brisk pace.

Mac calculated they had covered two city blocks when the tunnel again ended. This time a heavy steel door required their combined efforts to open. "Brogan helped me coming the other way. This entrance completely avoids the crowds outside the building." They put full strength into moving the barrier, then stepped into a brightly lit corridor.

A police officer in full combat gear confronted them. Amara talked with him briefly and he let Mac pass after checking his ID. A few hundred steps down the hallway, they boarded an elevator, and as they disembarked found themselves approaching the entrance to the United Nations General Assembly Hall.

Mac stopped to take in the scene before approaching the security guards controlling the entrance. Throngs of delegates streamed toward the large doors leading into the assembly space. Mac wondered how the people working here could struggle day after day to maintain order in a world gone half-mad.

Jim Brogan, wearing a suit, white shirt, and red tie, interrupted him.

"Welcome Mac," Brogan said. "It's great to be together with you and Amara again. Because the UN building is not technically American territory, CIA and Interpol agents will supplement the regular UN security force for this meeting. A few of us have even been cleared to carry firearms because the stakes are so high." He patted his shoulder holster. "A Glock is sometimes reassuring."

He handed Mac an earpiece. "This earbud-microphone combo is part of our secure communication system." He fitted it around Mac's right ear. "Please wear it in case you need to contact me urgently. Amara already has hers in place."

He looked over at Amara, who nodded and touched her ear under her luxurious dark hair.

"And now," Brogan asked, "Shall we go in?" He showed his creds to the security guards and led Amara and Mac into the General Assembly Hall.

Mac stood at the back of the chamber, awestruck. The room sloped gradually downward for half the distance of a football field, with tiers of desks and chairs providing seats for delegates with headphones, microphones, and country names. The presidential rostrum dominated center stage at the bottom, with a huge screen on either side. The speaker's marble podium stood on a platform below it. Galleries for visitors and observers were all empty because today's meeting was closed to the public.

People of every color, shape, and national dress chatted as delegates flowed into the hall. Their conversations created only a slight buzz in the cavernous space. Mac knew the UN held the hope that the nations of the earth could live in peace. The easy conversations taking place in front of him suggested that possibility might become reality.

A sense of anticipation hung in the air. Perhaps today, Mac thought, the urging of the two most influential presidents in the world would begin NoFear control and increase the status of the UN as a force for good.

"Impressive, isn't it?" Brogan asked. "Representatives from 193 countries trying to make the world a better place. But this space could hold danger. Look for example at those booths up in the aerie. They're supposed to hold translators, but who keeps them safe?"

"I assume you do," Mac said.

"We're trying to. We've instituted tight screening procedures for all the people who get into them, and I've asked our best people to patrol the corridor outside. And by the way, Amara is one of my best people. Although Interpol officers don't routinely carry guns, I arranged for her to be armed for this occasion. She certainly knows how to handle a firearm from her early police experience in Tangier."

Brogan drew Mac back from the foot traffic and pointed to the front of the room. "As a speaker, you'll be sitting in the front row of that cluster of seats." He pointed at about forty chairs arranged just below the stage on the left. "Members of the press and a few other invited guests will be behind you. The morning has already included speeches from experts and delegates. You're the third five-minute speaker in the afternoon schedule. Sterling Underwood will talk after you, then the Presidents will speak."

"I remember Underwood from the congressional hearing," Mac said. "He argued that NoFear is perfectly safe, that it has helped millions of people with anxiety, and that our entire freedom is at stake if the government tries to restrict it. He must know those are all lies. I don't understand how he can spout them with a straight face."

"Never underestimate the power of money," Brogan said. "We suspect Underwood's paid by both Chinese and Russian handlers but haven't been able to prove it. He seems to be a special supplier of NoFear to the rich and famous. Not an honorable person."

He pointed at the doors to the left of the stage. "Anyway, after he finishes, the Chinese and American presidents and their security guards will enter through those doors. They'll give their speeches at the podium, perhaps even together, then be escorted out the same way they entered."

"And where will you be during all this?" Mac asked.

"Wandering around the room trying to spot trouble-makers. There are a dozen security agents in plain clothes sprinkled through the crowd. We don't have intel about any specific disruptions, but with high-profile leaders like this it's our job to be prepared for the worst. I hope you'll be part of our surveillance group. Keep your eyes open and use the earpiece I gave you if you see anything suspicious."

不怕

CHAPTER FORTY-EIGHT

UNDERWOOD ARRIVES AT THE UN

MANHATTAN, NY

Karpov had warned Underwood about traffic delays on the day of the UN hearings, threatening that he must not be late for any reason. He advised Underwood to take a water taxi rather than land transportation to the UN building, then noted that he, Karpov, would not attend the meeting.

As always, Underwood did just what his handler ordered him to do.

The ride in the water taxi was pleasant. Sunlight reflected from the high-rise buildings of midtown Manhattan. A fresh breeze blew over the East River. A constant hum from FDR Drive provided an ostinato to horn blasts from tugboats and other vessels.

Approaching the docking site for the UN, Underwood considered the role he was about to play in history. The elimination of both Chinese and American presidents would produce world-wide chaos. That would mean more Russian influence in the American government, which should make him a very rich man. Karpov was paying him a lot of money now and had promised even more. Although the Chinese had recruited him to lobby for NoFear, and although they thought they were still his controllers, he had moved to an entirely different pay scale with Russia.

Underwood felt confident he could carry out this mission safely and continue his duplicitous role as long as he chose to. In the past, the idea of using a toxin to assassinate the Presidents of China and the United States would have filled him with terror. His own NoFear use changed all that. Now the project was just another challenge.

He steeled himself as he moved through the crowd toward the security station at the UN entrance. With the weapons of assassination in his pocket, he could not give off the vibes of a man with a deadly secret. As the security guards checked his ID and letter of invitation, he focused on various faces in the crowd around him, wondering who they were and why they were there.

He passed through the screening without incident. A few minutes later, he stood in the men's bathroom putting on his flesh-colored gloves. The toxin rested in a tube in his pocket, ready to be smeared on the gloves just before he had to speak.

Moving to his designated seat below the stage on the left, Sterling Underwood, assassin, folded his hands in his lap and waited for the meeting to begin.

不怕

CHAPTER FORTY-NINE

MAC SPEAKS TO THE UNITED NATIONS GENERAL ASSEMBLY

UN BUILDING, MANHATTAN

Five minutes before the meeting was scheduled to start, the UN General Secretary asked everyone to be seated and Mac moved to his designated area. There were three other men already in the row: a Turkish diplomat, a pharmaceutical expert, and Underwood.

The Turkish speaker minimized his country's initial role in the manufacture of NoFear, pointing out that Chinese and American operatives had begun producing it in Istanbul without governmental knowledge. He announced Türkiye had since then eliminated this compound and urged other countries to do the same. Mac joined heartily in the applause that followed.

The pharmaceutical representative argued that many countries had copied the United States in choosing not to regulate dietary supplements. He saw no reason that policy should change, pointing out that the FDA had more than enough to do screening real medications. By these criteria, no restriction should apply to NoFear.

Mac was invited to the podium next. "Let's clear up one misunderstanding from the start," he said. "NoFear is more than a dietary supplement. It is an addictive psychoactive drug which leads to irresponsible behavior and violence. Several months ago, I covered the emergency room at a suburban hospital near Boston. We were flooded with teenagers who had taken too much NoFear at a party. One had a seizure, one threw up and almost died on her own vomit, and a third required emergency brain surgery because she jumped from a stair landing. These were normal nice kids wrecked by this drug. And that was just one party's worth of NoFear victims. Imagine it occurring in thousands of other cities."

There was a murmur from the delegates that Mac allowed to swell.

"Fear is a gift," he continued, "a protective mechanism that keeps us from doing stupid and dangerous things. NoFear makes us lose those protective measures."

He paused to let this concept sink in, then went on to quote statistics of increased violence and chaotic behavior after NoFear appeared in the Unites States.

"Finally," he said, "You might wonder, *Why ask the United Nations to control this drug?* The answer is simple. The usual regulatory agencies here in America have bogged down in politics. The UN must now take the lead in NoFear management just as it did with COVID-19. Only you can make the world regulate NoFear. The life of someone in your own family may depend on it."

Enthusiastic applause echoed as he returned to his seat.

Sterling Underwood moved up to the podium and seemed almost to caress it with his hands. He rubbed the edges over and over as he downplayed the addictive element of NoFear and its tendency to lead to violence. He argued it was not a drug but simply a food supplement which had helped millions of people suffering from crippling anxiety. He read a few letters from patients extolling its virtues and finished with the claim that "freedom of choice has always been a cornerstone of democracy. A decision to take NoFear should be left to the individual. There should be no rules governing its distribution any more than vitamins should be regulated."

As Underwood concluded his speech, he raised his hand in a gesture of defiance against those who would limit individual freedom.

Mac blinked and then squinted to make sure his eyes were not playing tricks on him. Underwood's raised hand seemed to be covered with a flesh-colored glove.

不怕

CHAPTER FIFTY

THE HANDS OF STERLING UNDERWOOD

UNITED NATIONS BUILDING, MANHATTAN

A memory flashed into Mac's mind. Two years ago, a North Korean assassin had tried to murder him using a deadly poison smeared on her surgical gloves. He avoided death, but the experience left an indelible scar in his memory.

Mac's friend and CIA colleague James Brogan later explained that the woman was known for dispatching her victims with toxin absorbed through the skin. He added that this was still the weapon of choice for some Russian assassins.

Was Underwood wearing gloves to protect himself from a deadly toxin? Could he have smeared poison on the podium, hoping to kill two presidents who would grasp it after him? A crazy idea, but...

As Underwood returned to his seat, Mac confirmed that flesh-colored gloves protected his hands. The lobbyist did not try to remove the gloves but folded his hands in his lap like a choir boy waiting for something. A choir boy with a sly smile.

Mac whispered into the earpiece Brogan had given him. *Underwood's wearing gloves—could he have left toxin on the lectern?*

The opening of the left entrance door to the stage interrupted Mac. Eight security guards entered the chamber clustered around the Chinese and American leaders. Their path on the elevated stage passed in front of Mac four feet above the level of his seat.

Spontaneous applause erupted from the delegates as the presidents of China and the United States entered the hall. Many of the audience rose to their feet as they acknowledged the historic moment. Slowly, with the presidents waving and their individual security details surveying the surroundings, the group walked toward the podium.

Mac decided he had to take a chance. He leapt to his feet shouting, "Don't touch the podium," and raced toward the stairway that would take him to the stage.

Out of the corner of his eye, he saw Sterling Underwood, still wearing gloves, heading for the same stairs.

At Mac's words, the procession halted. Gasps and shouts erupted from the audience at the sudden commotion. In the presidents' cluster, seven security agents turned to retreat. The eighth, a man with a bald head, stood firm with his back to the hall, leaving a wide-open pathway in front of him for Underwood to get to the presidents as the group retreated toward the exit.

Mac realized that guard must be part of the assassination plot. He looked around for Brogan. A swarm of delegates blocked his view.

He had only a few seconds.

His vision tightened and reflexes became hyperacute. A cacophony of languages clashed around him. Delegates rushed toward the exits. Camera flashes erupted from the press section. The Secretary-General of the UN tried in vain to keep the audience under control, shouting to remain seated and stay calm.

Underwood reached the stairway. Mac realized that no observer would know he had a fatal chemical smeared on his gloves. Some might think he was trying to protect the presidents.

Mac pulled himself directly from the floor up onto the stage. The bald agent stood between him and Underwood's path to the presidents. Mac tackled the agent, pounding into him behind both knees. The guard's legs folded, and he fell forward directly into Underwood's path.

Destabilized by the agent's fall as he moved toward the presidents, Underwood grabbed the man's shaved head with his gloved hands to steady himself. The agent collapsed on the floor with Mac grasping his legs, but Underwood recovered his balance and staggered forward toward the presidents.

Mac held firm to the bald security guard's legs. Face down on the stage floor after the tackle, he braced himself for what he knew would come next. The bone-crushing impact of UN security kneeling on his back and handcuffing his wrists behind him left him helpless. He could only twist his head to watch what was happening on the rest of the stage. His part in the fight was over.

The presidential cluster slowed as panicked delegates swarmed and obstructed the path to the left entrance door. Underwood blocked Mac's view, but it would be only seconds before he smeared presidents and security guards with his deadly toxin.

An ear-shattering ***WHACK*** filled the room.

Mac saw a cascade of blood and brain blossom from the back of Underwood's head, felt spatters of gray matter land on his own face, and smelled the familiar odor of fresh blood.

Underwood collapsed.

Delegates dived to the floor.

The room became momentarily silent, then erupted into screams of terror.

Mac turned his head away from Underwood's lifeless body to see who had taken the shot.

In the periphery of his vision, Brogan stood resolute and grim in an aisle, displaying his CIA badge in one hand and a Glock in the other.

All hell broke loose as Brogan ran up onto the stage and shouted to the security guards rushing toward him. "That man was an assassin." He looked down at Mac. "I'll get you free in a minute. I hope to God you're right about the toxin."

"There's your proof," Mac said, nodding toward the agent he had tackled. "Underwood's hands touched this man's head, and scalp blood vessels absorb toxin quickly."

As they watched, the guard writhed on the floor, arched his back, foamed at the mouth, and died.

"I don't know how you figured this one out, but thank you," Brogan said to Mac. He waved his pistol at the crowd jamming the exit. "Get out of the way. We need to get the presidents out of the hall. And don't touch any part of the man with the blasted head."

The secret service agents still standing created a human shield around the presidents and pressed toward the exit. An Asian agent in the rear of the cluster turned back toward the hall with his pistol drawn to cover their departure.

His forehead exploded.

For a moment Brogan stood open-mouthed, then seemed to realize what had happened even though there had been no audible gunshot.

"Shooter!" he yelled. "Everybody stay down!"

不怕

CHAPTER FIFTY-ONE

SNIPER

UNITED NATIONS BUILDING, MANHATTAN

Brogan realized he faced a sniper who must be executing Plan B to assassinate the leaders of China and the United States. Plan A, the toxin, had definitely failed.

His heart raced as he scanned the assembly hall. Sweat ran into his eyes.

The Secretary-General and associates had taken cover behind their marble table. Mac lay unmoving, face-down but exposed on the stage with two security guards and Underwood lying dead beside him. A few people crowded to the stage exit trying to escape. The majority of delegates crouched under their tables in the main hall.

Brogan spotted a rifle barrel with suppressor protruding through the fractured window of translator's booth one. He peppered the booth with bullets as he followed the presidential security forces and remaining delegates through the exit.

He slammed the door shut behind him and moved away from the high velocity slugs now slamming into it, mentally visualizing the layout of the hall. No surprise that the booth with the shooter was the one meant for Russian translators.

"Amara, where are you?" he whispered into his communication headset.

"The corridor outside the translators' booths," she answered. "Where's the shooter?"

"Number one, the Russian booth."

Reloading his Glock, he whipped open the door and raced toward Mac, again covering the assassin's booth with shots as he crossed the stage. Reaching Mac safely, he dragged him to a position behind the podium, and waited coiled beside him.

A loud gunshot echoed across the hall, followed by the sound of shattered glass. Brogan glanced around the podium to see a body fall from the Russian translator's window and smash onto a delegates' desk thirty feet below.

Amara stood at the broken window of the booth. Her thumbs-up gesture showed she had carried out her mission, but there was no smile associated with it.

Brogan raced to the body of the would-be assassin, crumpled on the desk with limbs at crazy angles. "Who hired you?" he asked, staring into the terrified eyes of a dying man. Bloody froth bubbled from the assassin's mouth and he stopped breathing as Brogan watched.

Useless.

Delegates began to raise their heads. Brogan heard voices in many languages.

"*Was ist passiert?*"

"*Que pasa?*"

"*Qu'est-ce qu'il ya?*"

"Are we safe now?"

"Stay down, shelter in place until we get an all clear," Brogan shouted, standing beside the dead assassin, "except for the person with keys to Dr. MacGregor's cuffs. Whoever that is, get up here right away."

A UN security guard hustled to the stage and uncuffed Mac, who speedwalked with Brogan to a safe room just beyond the exit.

"The sniper must have thought I was dead," Mac said.

"Thank God you're not," Brogan said. "If you hadn't spotted Underwood's gloves and realized what they meant, we would be in a very different situation right now." He squeezed Mac's arm. "Stay here. I need to sweep the hall with security agents to be sure there are no other surprises. Be back in fifteen minutes."

When he returned after giving the all-clear, delegates and the press quickly filled the room. Journalists and social media reporters headed toward Mac and Brogan, flashing cameras, shouting questions, transmitting videos from smartphones held high...

"Let's get out of here," Brogan said.

"Lead on," Mac said. "How are you doing after all this?"

"I don't know yet" Brogan said. "My heart's still rattling. I'm just glad you were here."

不怕

CHAPTER FIFTY-TWO

CLOSING THE CASE

BEACON CLUB, BOSTON

Five weeks after the UN meeting, Mac organized dinner with Brogan at Boston's Beacon Club, an 1852 Beacon Hill landmark maintained through the centuries in excellent condition. Mac enjoyed its tranquil and discrete ambience and thought it would be a perfect place to catch up.

He waited for Brogan in the blue sitting room, relaxing beside the fireplace in an overstuffed chair. He had already added a seat for Brogan, who appeared in the doorway exactly at six.

"May I ask a favor?" Brogan said as he shook Mac's hand. "A friend would like to join us for a couple of minutes."

"As long as he or she is properly dressed," Mac said. "You know the rules. For men, jackets, ties, leather shoes; for women, no jeans or—"

Brogan's laughter stopped him cold. "I suggest you screen her yourself," Brogan said and stepped aside.

Amara Zadi, dazzling in a dark blue skirt and jacket complemented by a white silk blouse and Manolo Blahnik shoes, stepped into the room.

"Amara!" Mac said, rising to embrace her. He flashed back to their first meeting in Morocco, where they uncovered an ancient compound called Berserker in an adventure reaching from Tangier to Paris. She had joined Interpol after that and, following the UN episode, had returned to headquarters in Lyon, France.

"What brings you to Boston?" Mac asked. "Will you join us for dinner?"

"Sorry I can't. I have to get back to New York tonight."

Mac pulled up a third armchair and they clustered in front of the crackling fire.

"The United Nations shooting changed me." Amara said. "In Interpol, we don't do hands-on police work. We collect data. During the NoFear episode at the UN, I realized how much I miss field action. I decided to apply to the United Nations Police Force. I'm here for interviews, and New York is just an air shuttle jump away from Boston."

"As is D.C." Brogan added, "so this was the perfect meeting place."

"And is your family still thriving?" Mac asked. "I can't thank your father enough for endowing my professorship."

"The family is all healthy, and he's honored to have his name associated with your university."

"Will it be harder for them if you're in New York rather than Lyon?"

"Maybe harder, but they'll have a lot more fun when they visit."

"You were so important at the UN," Mac said. "Saved our lives and many others."

"Including the presidents of both the United States and China," Brogan added.

"Did you find out how the sniper got through security?" Amara asked.

"As part of the cleaning crew the day before. He hid overnight before the outside security was tightened."

"It was great to be part of the team again," Amara said,

"but I hope assassination attempts aren't routine at General Assembly meetings."

"The UN is our future," Mac said. "Consider what happened with NoFear. No single country was willing to ban it because of local corruption and lobbying efforts. After the United Nations resolution to make it illegal, even the U.S. was shamed into acting."

Brogan nodded his head. "It was amazing how quickly that resolution passed after UN delegates saw for themselves what NoFear could do, when they were told that Underwood took it."

"Of course, the problem will be enforcing the ban," Amara said. "Interpol will collect information about where NoFear is being manufactured and sold, but it's going to be up to individual countries to block it."

She looked at her smartwatch and rose from her chair. "My ride is here. May we meet again soon."

"*Inshallah*," Mac and Brogan said almost in unison as she shook hands and left.

"I hope we'll be seeing more of her if she gets the job," Brogan said. "I told the security chief at the UN they would be crazy not to hire her." He looked at his watch. "But can we discuss the rest over Dover Sole? I should leave for Logan in about an hour to get last shuttle to D.C."

They sat at a secluded table in a spacious dining room furnished with ornate dark wood and elegant chandeliers.

"So Russia was behind both assassination attempts at the UN?" Mac asked.

"No question, "Brogan said. "It was the Russian toxin *Novichok* that Underwood smeared on the podium, and the sniper was a well-known operative for the Russian Foreign Intelligence Service. His primary job was probably to kill

Underwood once the presidents were dead. His attempted shooting of the presidents themselves may have been an improvisation."

"Is Underwood's handler still alive?" Mac asked.

"The guy was Viktor Karpov, an oligarch living in New York. He fell to his death from the window of his Manhattan condo two weeks ago. Russian justice is a little more brutal than ours."

A server presented Dover Sole under silver covers and added rice and roasted vegetables from a serving tray. Conversation paused, turned to families and jobs, and then resumed once macaroons and flan appeared as dessert.

"What about the original plan to manufacture NoFear as a bioweapon?" Mac asked. "Was that concocted by Russia?"

"China." Brogan said. "Han Li, a senior member of the Politburo, was the mastermind. His body was found floating in the Chang Jiang River three weeks ago. China appears to have no further interest in NoFear. Like all other countries in the United Nations except Russia, it has outlawed the drug."

"So NoFear as a threat is finished?"

"I hope so." As he finished his coffee, he added, "This whole saga reminds me how complicated warfare is today, Mac. You and I have faced a lot together. In the past, we knew what the weapons were."

Mac nodded. "Today, a weapon can be almost anything—a dietary supplement, social media, the law—the list gets longer and longer. I guess the important thing is to recognize what's being used as a weapon when we see it."

"And with that, I'm out of here." Brogan said, rising from his chair. "Thanks for a great dinner. May our paths cross soon."

不怕

EPILOGUE

HUBEI PROVINCE, CHINA

Two months after meeting with Brogan, Mac received an invitation to return to Wuhan China at the request of Dr. Feng Meixiu. Dr. Feng had been Mac's doctor in Wuhan when he contracted COVID-19 before its worldwide spread. She had risen to become the executive vice-president of the Zhongyang Hospital and a senior official in the communist party.

He discussed the proposed week in China at the dinner table.

"Are you going to get COVID-19 again?" his daughter Maggie asked,

"Can you bring us back something great to show in class?" his son Peter asked.

"Please don't turn a week into three months again," his wife Lauren said.

The next day, Mac accepted Feng's invitation on the condition that he also visit the Three Gorges Dam, a four-hour car ride from Wuhan. Sophie Grainger had told him this was where the saga of NoFear began.

Feng thanked him profusely. "You are a hero for our city. You helped us manage COVID-19 with the protocols and procedures you designed after you recovered from the disease yourself. I speak for the hospital and entire city in extending my invitation. And we can certainly journey to Three Gorges while you are here. I have not visited that region for years and would be delighted to see it again."

Feng met Mac at the Wuhan airport and transported him to the beautiful Wanda Reign Hotel, where he had previously stayed. To adjust to the twelve-hour time difference between Beijing and Boston, he walked around the Wuhan University campus again. It was now filled with students and families enjoying nature without restriction, very different from the deserted campus he had seen as he left the city three years ago.

Official events occupied the second day—a tour of the city, lunch with city officials, and a visit to the Zhongyang Hospital.

The tour showed that the ghost city Mac had left during the quarantine period was now very much alive. Streets bustled with vendors, workers, bicyclists, and shoppers. The Wuhan Institute of Virology was active with a new chief. The Wuhan Huanan Seafood Wholesale Market, possibly the initial propagator of COVID-19, remained permanently closed and guarded as a reminder of the past.

Mac and Feng enjoyed a sumptuous luncheon with city officials that included dim sum, Six Delights noodle soup, and many seafood dishes. The talks that followed the luncheon were difficult for Mac to follow even though Feng translated as fast as she could.

"Thank you all," Feng said after the sixth city official had proclaimed how important Mac had been to their recovery. "And now we must leave. We should be at Zhongyang hospital by two p.m."

"Is there some reason we have to be there by two?" Mac asked as Feng and he left the banquet hall together.

"Perhaps," Feng said with a slight smile.

They arrived at the plaza in front of the hospital at exactly two o'clock.

Mac noted two statues he had not seen on his previous visit.

One memorialized Dr. Chow, a woman who had tried to warn the government and her fellow physicians about the pandemic and then mysteriously disappeared.

The second...

Mac stared at it, not understanding. The statue looked very much like *him*.

Dozens of doctors, nurses, students, and technicians poured through the hospital's front entrance and surrounded Mac as he stood with a quizzical frown.

"I'll translate the inscription for you," Feng said with a grin.

"*This statue is dedicated to Dr. Duncan MacGregor, who survived COVID-19 in Wuhan and helped our city do the same.*"

He was flooded with memories of his bout with COVID three years before, how sick he felt, how grateful he was for the work of the doctors who took care of him. He also remembered his hours helping the city and hospital administrators create protocols for prevention and treatment as he himself was recovering from the virus.

The crowd applauded and cheered as Feng read the citation. Mac was touched by both the applause and the memorial itself. With tears wetting the corners of his eyes, he thanked the people assembled, pointing out with a quavering voice that they had saved his life.

"Sorry about the surprise," Feng said after the crowd dispersed. "I really meant it when I said you helped us all get through the COVID crisis. Now we must prepare for tomorrow's trip to Three Gorges."

Early the next morning, Mac and Feng boarded the train from Wuhan to Yichang. Riding in a first-class coach, they luxuriated in a compartment with red velvet seats and a cabinet stocked with green tea and Chinese pastries. The humming of the wheels and swaying of the train created a hypnotically delightful background to their conversation, heightened by the verdant countryside passing by the windows.

As the train built up to its high speed, Feng described the Three Gorges Dam they were about to see. "It's an engineering marvel, the world's largest dam project. At first many local citizens demonstrated against it because it flooded some of the most beautiful landscapes of Northwestern China. It displaced a million people, submerged thirteen cities and one hundred forty towns."

She sipped her tea. "On the positive side, it has controlled the overflow of the Chang Jiang River, which you might know better as the Yangtze. Regular flooding of the river used to cost many lives, and the dam has provided the region with electricity equal to twenty of your Hoover Dams. It has become a symbol of China's power in the most literal sense."

She rested back on the plush velvet and said, "I've told you about the dam. Now please tell me about the *Bupa* plant and why you wanted to take this trip."

"The *Bupa* plant was transformed into a drug called NoFear by an American scientist named Sophie Grainger,"

Mac said. "It destroyed her and almost destroyed both the United States and China."

"It made a lot of trouble in Wuhan too. Why is it so bad?"

"The drug makes people do crazy things because they lose the restraints provided by a sense of fear. And it is addictive. It created havoc everywhere it was distributed. The United Nations and World Health Organization classified it with heroin and outlawed it in all countries including the United States. Law enforcement agencies around the world are now working to destroy manufacturing facilities and eliminate its distribution."

"That's already happened in China. Our government has the power to control such things. How will limiting this drug work in more liberal systems?"

"There's still a lot to do, especially in the United States where even now some people want to keep it. However, following the advice of the UN, the American Food and Drug Administration has classified it with heroin, a drug with no medical use and serious potential for abuse."

As the train rocked gently, he closed his eyes and considered the disasters associated with NoFear. He wanted to remember and acknowledge them.

As a shrill whistle blew, he jerked awake again. "NoFear did help the world in one way," he said as if he had been talking all along. "It strengthened the United Nations as a world force for medical issues. The disgraceful denial of NoFear's dangers by American congressmen and government officials demonstrated that only an outside force like the UN could tell the truth."

"We've arrived in Yichang," Feng said. "I hope you enjoyed your nap."

They ate lunch at the Great Hall of the People.

Mac asked Feng to track down the herbalist Sophie told him about in the first days of NoFear. The old woman was not cordial after Feng explained in Mandarin what they were looking for. “I remember that American,” she said. “I told her the *Bupa* plant was forbidden and she should leave it alone. She seemed to be the kind of person who would not listen. I hope she followed my advice.”

“Sadly, she didn’t,” Mac commented. “And it cost her life. Do you still keep *Bupa* in your garden?”

“Not possible. I would be arrested by the police.”

They returned to the taxi stand. “Why did you want to see that woman?” Feng asked.

“Maybe a sense of completeness in remembering Sophie,” Mac said. He stepped into a flower store and bought three white orchids before they climbed into a taxi to transport them to the Three Gorges site.

When they got to the dam, Feng arranged for the taxi to stay in the lot reserved for VIPs and led Mac to the observation platform.

Nothing prepared him for what he saw. A concrete and steel structure stretching more than a mile across the gorge backed up the Chang Jiang River to a height of five hundred feet. The roar of the water, spray of mist against his face, and huge sluices delivering tons of water every second almost drowned every sense.

Mac remembered Sophie’s account of dangling above the roiling water, twisting and turning as a stranger saved her from suicide. *What would have happened if he had not intervened, if NoFear had not been produced?* he thought as he looked at the cascading currents.

He strode quickly along the walkway to an area above the dam without tourists or pounding water, then dropped his orchids one by one into the quiet reservoir.

One for Hassan.

One for Sophie.

And one for all other victims of NoFear, hopefully its final casualties.

THE END

不怕

AUTHOR'S COMMENTS

In this book, I have tried to describe some of the neuroscientific foundations of fear and potential consequences of eliminating it.

An important subtheme of the story is the use of non-traditional weapons in the struggle for democracy. Denial, lies, corruption in the courts and media, perversion of law, social media manipulation, even health food supplements can be weapons in undeclared war we face against tyranny. We must recognize them as weapons to defend ourselves against them.

We can only manage the potential disasters facing our world by caring for, learning from, and collaborating with each other. The United Nations is an imperfect model for doing this, but it may be the best chance we have.

This novel would not have been written without the support of Carole Holladay, to whom I owe an ongoing debt.

Hans and Judy Copek, Cheryl Lawton Malone, Carol Lynn, and Sean Harding offered almost weekly guidance for the early drafts. Michael Abram, Sally Tripple, Christopher Black, Dorian Mintzer, and Alex Malozemoff were instrumental in guiding the revisions made to the final text.

Mayapriya Long of Bookwrights designed the book and cover and I am grateful for her ability and kindness.

I am especially grateful to you as reader or listener. You make the effort of writing worthwhile.

Peter Black
London
August 2024

THE AUTHOR

Dr. Peter Black has been a physician to Congress and the Supreme Court, Professor of Neurosurgery at Harvard Medical School, and President of the World Federation of Neurosurgical Societies.

NoFear is the fourth book in his Duncan MacGregor thriller series. *Seizure*, the first in the series, won the *Writer's Digest* prize for best indie genre fiction of 2021. (Genre fiction includes mysteries, thrillers, westerns, and romance.)

All four books—*Seizure, Death by Denial, Berserker,* and *NoFear,* are available on Amazon in ebook, paperback, hardcover, and audiobook versions.

Dr. Black divides his time between Boston and London, tending to his grandchildren and gardens. He enjoys spending time with his own family and his wonderful life partner and her family, reading books, and attending concerts and theater when he's not writing. He can be tracked down on the web at peterblackbooks.com, on Facebook and Instagram as peterblackbooks, and on X as @peterblackbooks2. The best way to find him on Amazon is to search for Dr. Peter Black.

Milton Keynes UK
Ingram Content Group UK Ltd.
UKHW030626071224
451790UK00020B/144/J

9 781952 683152